TWEAKED

TWEAKED

KATHERINE HOLUBITSKY

ORCA BOOK PUBLISHERS

Library and Archives Canada Cataloguing in Publication

Holubitsky, Katherine
Tweaked / written by Katherine Holubitsky.

ISBN 978-1-55143-851-1

I. Title.

PS8565.O645T84 2008   jC813'.54   C2007-907382-4

First published in the United States, 2008

Library of Congress Control Number: 2007942242

Summary: Gord is powerless to stop his brother's drug addiction from destroying his family.

Orca Book Publishers gratefully acknowledges the support for its publishing programs provided by the following agencies: the Government of Canada through the Book Publishing Industry Development Program and the Canada Council for the Arts, and the Province of British Columbia through the BC Arts Council and the Book Publishing Tax Credit.

Cover and text design by Teresa Bubela

ORCA BOOK PUBLISHERS   ORCA BOOK PUBLISHERS
PO Box 5626, STN. B   PO Box 468
VICTORIA, BC CANADA   CUSTER, WA USA
V8R 6S4   98240-0468

www.orcabook.com
Printed and bound in Canada.
Printed on 100% PCW paper.

11 10 09 08 • 4 3 2 1

For my sister, Mary

ACKNOWLEDGMENTS

I am grateful to my editor, Sarah Harvey, for her insight, eagle-eye and above all, her support.

ONE

When my brother, Chase, was twelve and I was eleven he built a tepee in the ravine behind our house. He followed the instructions in an old book from the 1930s that he'd found at my grandmother's. It was called *How to Survive in the Woods* or something like that. It covered everything from skinning a deer and tanning the hide to constructing different types of shelters.

Every day for two weeks during the summer holidays, Chase hoisted an ax onto his shoulder and walked down into the ravine. I went with him for the first couple of hours on the first day, but it was boring, and I ended up coming home and playing with my friends. Every night at dinner, Dad would ask Chase how his project was going.

Chase told him it was going very well. Until, on the Friday evening of the second week he answered, "I need to get some unbleached Egyptian cotton."

Dad laughed. "Unbleached Egyptian cotton, okay. Tomorrow I'll take you to a fabric store."

Mom told us which store would likely have what Chase wanted and so, on the Saturday morning, the three of us guys drove off. Dad was not particularly comfortable in the fabric store. He had no idea what he was looking for, but the clerk was very helpful. After asking what the unbleached Egyptian cotton was for, she found a bolt of creamy white fabric.

"Can I paint it?" Chase asked.

"Paint it?" she repeated as she flipped several yards of cloth onto the cutting table.

"Yes, it's going to be authentic. I'm going to paint the designs and symbols that are in the book."

The clerk winked at Dad who smiled. "Why, yes, we have fabric paints that will work just fine."

Chase seemed satisfied with this.

"Now, how much do you need?" she asked.

Chase referred to the scrap of paper that he pulled from his pocket. "Two hundred and fifty yards."

Dad looked at Chase and laughed while the clerk smiled. She then gently told him that he must be mistaken, and anyhow there were only twenty yards on the bolt. But Chase was insistent. Finally Dad told the clerk we'd be back once he'd calculated the correct amount himself, and we left the store.

Once at home, I ran ahead of Chase while Dad followed us into the ravine. I jumped the dried-up creek bed twenty yards into the woods and headed up the hill. Standing at the top, looking down into the little valley where all of us kids in the neighborhood played and built forts, I couldn't believe my eyes. A family of beavers couldn't have destroyed so many trees in two weeks. Stripped of their bark, twenty or so trees stood lashed together around a central tripod in a new clearing. Chase was building the real thing.

Dad was furious. He marched back to the house with Chase in tow while I ran in and around the frame of the tepee.

Later that night our neighbor, Mrs. Goodman, knocked on the door. She'd been walking her dog down in the ravine and she'd come across the destruction. She'd also seen Chase and me leave the house with an ax, and she demanded to know what on earth was going on.

I am remembering all of this as I sit on the bus on my way to the hospital to visit a man I've never met. My brother, Chase, put him in the hospital. Chase has been arrested for aggravated assault. I have been trying to figure out how things got so out of control. There must be a reason why Chase turned out the way he did. I wonder if someone crushed his dreams, or perhaps his dreams were just so big and outrageous they were impossible to achieve and so he simply gave up.

Chase is an A-head—a serious crystal methamphetamine user. The police told us he had been awake for days, maybe as many as seven, when he struck the man with a bottle. He was tweaking, looking for another hit to level him off. The guy he sent to the hospital was a parking meter reader, a stranger.

Over the past two years, there have been many times when I have seen Chase like that. Hyped up, pupils flickering in his head like a pinball machine, skin yellow-gray, sores festering all over his face. Ready to fight anyone who comes near him because he's suddenly got it in his head that everyone is out to get him: fists clenched, no muscle left in his 130-pound body, but every stringy sinew stretched taut.

A shop owner taking out his garbage found the guy and called the police. When they pulled up, Chase was slumped against the wall with the neck of the broken bottle still clutched in his hand. He didn't put up a struggle or even grumble much when they cuffed him.

In fact, when the two police officers arrived at our door yesterday morning to tell us all this, they said Chase was so ready to crash he couldn't keep his eyes open on the way to the police station.

Once they'd explained the charge, Dad sighed heavily, although he showed little surprise.

Mom, on the other hand, looked between the two men with wide eyes. "Aggravated assault?" she repeated.

"Oh, no, you've got the wrong boy. It couldn't be Chase."

After all that has happened, she still reacts like it's a real stretch of the imagination that Chase could do anything wrong. Although, to be fair, I think it has become a sort of self-defense. It's like she hears a terrible crash, so she throws her hands in front of her face, not wanting to see the accident. Then, once the sound fades, she pulls her hands away slowly while she gets accustomed to the bloodiness of the scene.

Once the police left, she began pulling drawers in and out. "Get your keys," she told Dad. "We're going down to the police station." She slammed cupboard doors open and shut. "I mean, he obviously wasn't in his right mind. Isn't there a defense for that?" She continued to search the kitchen. I knew what she was looking for—her purse.

For a year and a half, Mom and Chase had played their own crazy version of cat and mouse. Mom had hidden her purse in every conceivable place in the house, but Chase had always found it. She had hidden it so often and in so many places, even she couldn't remember where she'd last put it. "Oh, forget it." She gave up. "Let's just go."

The story was in the back pages of the newspaper this morning. Dad quickly scanned it. He was relieved that because Chase is one month short of his eighteenth birthday he wasn't named. He was the *seventeen-year-old suspect of no fixed address* in custody.

The no-fixed-address part is true unless they give street numbers to stairwells and Dumpsters. Dad had booted him out of the house six months ago when the stealing got so bad we had to nail the furniture down.

Dad passed the article to Mom. She cried quietly as she read it. How many times can a heart be broken? she wanted to know. Dad reminded her that they would do everything in their power to get Chase out of it. He then said that maybe it was even a good thing—a blessing in disguise. It might force him to get the help he really needs.

I picked up the paper and read the article myself. One thing was for sure, it was no blessing for Richard Cross. He was the guy in intensive care. Neither of my parents had even mentioned the man Chase had smashed on the head.

Richard Cross was working, taking his usual shortcut through the alley when Chase brought him down. The police said the motive wasn't clear because the man's money pouch was still around his waist after he was attacked. His injuries are life threatening and his condition is listed as critical. And like a blunt object it hit *me*. "He might die."

I felt both Mom's and Dad's eyes on me before I realized that I'd said it out loud. "Yes, we know," Dad said. "That worries us too. Things will be very bad for Chase if he does."

At that moment I could no longer stay in the same room as them. I didn't know them anymore. Two years of living with Chase the addict had turned them into strangers. I thought I understood my parents, their morals and what they valued. After all, hadn't I learned my own values from them? But Chase has stretched and twisted those values until they are a tangled mess, and I am hanging on to mine by the thinnest of wires.

Half an hour later I headed out the door. I am now sitting on the bus. We pass Barnes Hardware store, where I work. The hospital is still another ten blocks.

When we were young and sharing the back-seat of the car on road trips, Chase and I used to play Hangman and Red Car. I can still remember when we played Red Car for the last time. Dad had just pulled into a gas station when Chase spotted one of those big old Chryslers from the seventies. "Red car!" he yelled. "That's six for me and four for you."

"That's not red," I told him. "It's purple."

"It's red. Mom, what color is that car?"

Mom looked to where Chase pointed. "It's maroon. Sort of purple, but not really. A combination of red and brown, I think."

"See?" said Chase. "Red. A point for me."

I argued until Mom said, "Well, maybe Chase could have half a point. It does have red in it."

Chase grinned. "That's five and a half points for me."

When Dad pulled back onto the highway we started assigning half points for cars with any combination of red. Then it progressed to fractions of points if there was even a stroke of red: a letter, a symbol or a shape of some kind. We completely lost track of who had how many points and ended up arguing until Dad said if we didn't stop squabbling he was going to pull over right there and then and put us both out on the side of the road.

I get off the bus two blocks short of the hospital. I am hoping the walk will help build the confidence I need to do what I am about to do.

The lobby is bright and smells of disinfectant. The floor is still wet in places where it has been washed. Walking quickly, trying to appear as if I have every reason for being there, I approach the receptionist seated behind the information booth. She jots down the floor and number of Richard Cross's room for me.

The elevator reaches the right floor and the door opens. For a moment, I am not sure I have the guts to carry this off. But I know that if I don't do it, no one else is going to apologize on Chase's behalf. I force myself to step out of the elevator. "I'm Gordie Jessup," I tell the nurse on duty behind the desk on his unit. "Mr. Cross's nephew," I quickly add.

It surprises me how easily this lie has come into my head and out of my mouth. But it is a practical lie. Lucky for me there has been a shift change and because Richard Cross has only been in for one day, there seems to be some confusion as to who is family. When I ask, I am told he has no other visitors. The nurse then directs me down the hall.

With the exception of the rhythmic puffing and wheezing of the machines that are pumping stuff in and out of him, Mr. Cross's room is quiet, although the lights are ablaze. He is not conscious. I'm not sure why I thought he would be, but I now realize he won't hear my apology or anything I have come to say. Still, I sit in the one chair next to his bed.

I guess him to be roughly in his mid-thirties. His entire head, right down to his eyebrows, is swathed in a huge white bandage, like a giant wasp nest engulfing his head. I can't tell what color his hair is, or if he has any at all. His twenty-four-hour beard is dark, though, so I imagine his hair is too. I think it strange how his beard continues to grow while he lies there unaware of what has happened to him.

His face is calm and uninjured. Chase had whacked him from behind. On the wall across from where I sit, above Mr. Cross's bed, are taped two drawings. The one closest to me is a unicorn on a hill backed by a fringed sun. The other is a unicorn lying in a stable with a

Band-Aid on its head. They are drawn in crayon by a child. The one with the Band-Aid says, *Get better soon, Daddy*. Beneath the unicorn, in big, uneven letters are the words, *love Hannah*. The *n*'s are backward. Richard Cross has a little kid.

I look at Richard Cross, and I wonder again how it came to this.

At first only Chase was affected by his habit. He'd emptied his bank account and sold everything that he owned. Then Mom and Dad became involved, and me, of course. Any excuse to borrow money, anything we owned that he could pawn, he did. Once we'd wised up he started harassing Grandma and stealing from her before hitting on Mom's sister, Aunt Gail. Then there were the teachers at school who gave him every opportunity when he was flunking—make-up exams, special assignments, until he was finally kicked out. And now, Richard Cross, some guy he doesn't even know, is lying here in the hospital fighting for his life.

I think Richard Cross must be cold. His chest is exposed, with lots of tubes and instruments attached to it, monitoring his life. I am careful not to disturb any of them as I pull the extra blanket at his feet up to his waist.

"Gordie?"

I look up. The nurse I spoke to before is standing at the door. She is a redhead about Richard Cross's age. Her nametag says *Lisa*. I realize she is talking to me.

"You'll have to leave for a while. The doctor needs to see Mr. Cross."

"Yeah, sure." Swinging my backpack over my shoulder, I leave the room.

On my way back to the bus stop, it occurs to me how nobody lives the way my family does. My life is not normal. We hide everything that can be pawned or sold. My parents don't even keep wine in the house. Aspirin, painkillers and allergy tablets are out. It's a good thing none of us has a serious illness that requires medication, because we'd be out of luck.

Nobody I know worries about waking up in the middle of the night with a space cadet rummaging through their room, searching for money, credit cards, anything to get that next hit. Or to pay off drug debts. "You have no idea what they do to guys who don't pay," Chase whined at me at three o'clock one morning months ago. I was sacked out. I'd worked five shifts in a row, and exams were coming up. Chase was rooting through my drawers.

"Get out," I told him.

"But, Gordie," he whimpered, "I need sixty bucks right now. They're going to break my hands if I walk out that door without it."

He harasses my friends for money. He lies, he manipulates, and it's embarrassing. He's sick, Mom and Dad keep telling me. It's a disease. Try to be understanding until he's got it under control.

I am not convinced. Nobody stands there with a gun at his head, forcing him to smoke ice. Nobody runs him down and sticks a needle in his arm. Chase makes that decision every time he scores.

I have gone over everything I can think of and I've come to the conclusion that nobody mistreated him. Nobody crushed his dreams or did anything to Chase. Mom and Dad encouraged him and they taught him right from wrong. I just think that once Chase took that first hit he didn't want to stop.

TWO

I try to avoid talking to people in the days following Chase's arrest. My friend, Jack Bentz, says I'm crazy if I think that what Chase has done reflects on me, but I can't help but feel that it does.

It's Jade that gets me talking about it. She works in the same hardware store. She started working around the same time I did, but while I got the job so I could buy a new guitar, Jade got it so she could eat. She lives with her mother and her nine-year-old sister, Holly, and they're always broke.

Jade's mother has been sick for a very long time. I've been to her place only once, to drop off her paycheck when she couldn't get out. Mrs. Scott was lying on the shabby old couch in the living room of their apartment, all pale and sweaty, a tube running from her nose to an oxygen machine. "Her lungs fill up with fluid," Jade told me. "She coughs all the time, especially at night, and she can't leave the house without dragging the oxygen along."

In the six months I have known her, Jade has taken her mother to the hospital at least three times. Jade's father left after Holly was born. He couldn't deal with her mother's illness: the medications and treatments, the trips to the hospital. Jade never seems to blame him. She talks about him like she understands that not everyone can handle that kind of thing. Since he left, they've survived on the little disability money her mother receives.

Anyway, after all she's been through, I guess Jade is just really in tune with the way people are feeling. She seems to be able to sense when something is wrong.

"Oh, you must be just sick," she says after I tell her about going to see Richard Cross in the hospital.

That's one of the things I really like about her. She's never automatically assumed that because we are brothers that I am in any way like Chase.

"Wow," she says, delicately unwrapping a cheese sandwich. "Don't you wish you could turn back time? I bet your brother does. Twenty-four hours ago everything was so different."

"Not really," I say. "It's been coming to this for two years."

"He's been into drugs for two years?"

"Yeah, as far as I know."

"I'm sorry." She smiles as she squeezes my hand. "Hey, do you want a tart? When Mom's feeling up to it she loves to bake. She made about five dozen yesterday. I feel bad if I don't eat what she makes, so every couple of months I gain about fifteen pounds. She's actually quite amazing when she's feeling good, a virtual whirlwind. She cooks a pile of meals to freeze and she bakes; she has the apartment cleaned from top to bottom in the space of only a few hours."

"Thanks," I say, not only for the tart she passes me, but also for changing the subject so smoothly. "What kind are they?"

"What kind? Oh, she usually grinds up whatever she's throwing out of the fridge. I know there were some old Brussels sprouts I couldn't bring myself to cook for Holly and me."

I jerk the tart away from my mouth like I'm about to eat a toad. Jade laughs. "Gordie, I'm kidding! They're butter tarts. Go ahead. What are you doing this weekend?"

"Picking up my guitar. You know, the one I've been slaving away for by working here? I took it in to have the strings changed and some adjustments made. I can hardly wait to get it back." I bite into the tart.

"That is so cool," she says. "How's that tart?"

I nod as I chew. "Good. I could eat more than one. Which is more than I can say about Brussels sprouts, that's for sure."

For the rest of the afternoon we don't talk about Chase. Jade doesn't ask about how he got into drugs or

what it's been like living with him now. These are things
I would never tell her anyway, because the details are so
skuzzy that even I am revolted all over again every time
I look back on how Chase started on the road to where
he is now.

The first time Chase smoked ice, Mom and Dad had left
us alone over a three-day weekend. That was two years
ago. It was a non-stop party with every freaky friend
Chase could round up. Dad had left a hundred dollars
for stuff like milk, peanut butter and bread. Chase spent
it all on booze. To this day, I don't know how he got hold
of it; he was only sixteen. He spent three days drinking
and puking.

He skipped school on the Friday, so that by the time
I got home he was already smashed. "Hey, Gordie,"
he said, when I walked in the door. "Dinner's in the
cooler." His goofball friends laughed. I'm no prig, but
when I saw a smoldering cigarette butt lying on the
coffee table next to the ashtray, it hit me that I didn't
want to take the heat when Mom discovered the burn.
She'd go ballistic—after going back to work she'd spent
her first paychecks on new living room furniture.

I didn't know it was the first time Chase got into
meth. I found out later. I didn't know, because when I saw
what was going on, I stayed with Jack for the weekend.

I came home an hour before Mom and Dad arrived home. Chase and his friends had done a really lame job of cleaning the house. Two of the lightbulbs in the basement were broken and the pieces they hadn't used as pipes still lay on the floor. "Gordie did it," Chase told them, "playing basketball."

I gaped at him while he signaled for me to keep my mouth shut.

Over the next few months, he spent nearly every weekend at one friend's house or another. He'd started hanging out with a couple of real losers: Harris Reed and Ryan Linscott, guys Jack and I had voted most likely to become hit men. The two of them had been in trouble for one thing or another since they were in nursery school. Harris lived down the street from Jack. Their mothers worked in the same office, so I'd heard plenty of stuff through him.

A couple of months later, the calls started coming from school. Chase had missed biology. He'd missed the whole afternoon. He'd missed entire days. Chase was not going to pass the term. Then Mom found a pipe in his room.

"It's Harris's," he told her. "I didn't know he was into the stuff. When I discovered it, I stole it, hoping it would smarten him up. I've missed so much school because I've been trying to keep tabs on him."

Mom and Dad appeared skeptical.

"Look," said Chase, "if it was mine, do you think I'd be dumb enough to leave it out in the open?"

Of course not. One of their own children could never be that dumb.

Dad looked puzzled more than anything, while Mom was relieved. "Well," she began cautiously, "an addiction is not something to fool around with. Perhaps I should phone his mother. I know you're trying to help, dear, but it is beyond your experience."

Chase frowned, as though he was actually considering that she should. Finally he said, "I'm not sure that would be such a good idea. His parents are going through a divorce. They're kind of messed up right now. Don't worry, I've talked to the counselor at school."

Amazingly they believed him. Not only that, they congratulated him on being such a good friend. Still, Chase was not to hang around with Harris until he pulled himself together. He was also grounded on weeknights until his marks improved.

He managed to get around this by telling them he had to work with friends on group projects, he had to go to the library, or he had to practice if he was to make the soccer team.

Somehow he did make it through that term, even though he spent every weekend spun out. He was awake for thirty-six hours before exams, hyped up, cramming. He never made it through the next term, though.

By Christmas he hardly went to school at all. School was such a struggle, he sobbed to Mom and Dad. He just didn't get it. They gave him money for private tutoring and money for additional textbooks; it all went to his dealer. Chase would be flying for days, and then he wouldn't get out of bed for three in a row.

I never understood how Mom and Dad couldn't see that he was hooked, how they could be so naïve. It took me awhile to realize it was because they didn't want to see it. They made every excuse to avoid admitting that drugs were the reason he was in such bad physical shape. Or, maybe they truly believed their own excuses. I couldn't tell for sure. He was stressed-out over his failure at school; stress does terrible things to people. It prevented him from sleeping, and he couldn't eat, which is why he'd lost thirty pounds. They made appointments with the doctor; he never showed up.

Considering his poor grades, my parents knew it probably wasn't a good idea to allow Chase to go on the school trip to France over spring break that year. But he'd feel left out if they didn't, and perhaps the trip would inspire him to start working harder. They gave him a fifteen-hundred-dollar money order to take to school. Chase disappeared for three weeks. He went on a bender with his druggie friends. He was the ice man. They had a high time on the money that was meant to fly him to France.

My parents were frantic. They thought he'd run away or maybe even committed suicide because he was doing so badly at school. Then, for what would be the first of many times, the cops arrived at our door. Chase had been hauled out of a meth house and was charged with possession. Mom stumbled like someone had hit the back of her knees, and Dad was at a complete loss for words.

When they brought Chase home from the remand center, he looked like he'd been living in a trench. He smelled worse than an old rummy. His face was all broken out in crank craters, and he even had lice. Mom really flipped out when she saw the little white bugs crawling all over his scalp, dropping to his shoulders.

Once Chase had crashed, they confronted me.

"Gordie, how long has your brother been into drugs? And why on earth didn't you tell us?"

I was stunned. "Hey," I said, "I didn't know it was this bad. It's not like we pal around together. Besides, if he won't listen to you, what makes you think he'd listen to me?"

A look of confusion came over Dad's face. I suddenly felt bad. I hadn't meant to criticize him as a parent. From all comparisons I'd made with my friends' parents, he was a pretty good one, which I suppose was all the more reason why what I said was true.

Besides, what I couldn't tell them was that I had made my own attempts when I could see that he was straight enough to talk. But all I ever got for my efforts was a pat on the cheek and a patronizing "Gordie, it's all under control."

But then, what older brother listens to the younger kid? Chase was always the one who steered the bike when we rode double or wrenched the controls out of my hand when he got impatient playing video games. When I was ten, he talked me into going on the Zipper at the exhibition, even though I barely scraped past the minimum-height restriction. It was the first year our parents had dropped us off at the gate and allowed us to spend the day on our own.

"Stand on your tiptoes," Chase whispered once we got to the front of the line and he was able to eyeball the yellow tape on the side of the wicket. I did as I was told. I still don't think I quite reached it, but the guy in charge was distracted by a couple of girls and waved us through.

As we sat in the cage, waiting for the ride to start, I reminded Chase that I was afraid of heights.

"It's being scared that makes it fun. You'll see. Besides—" he rattled the cage, causing it to swing violently— "it's safe, and you'll be fine. You hardly ever hear of rides breaking down; they inspect them all the time. Just don't look down."

I quickly discovered that this was virtually impossible as we careened face-first in the cage toward the ground at a hundred miles an hour. I screamed—a long, heartfelt scream.

"Okay, so you have no choice but to look down." He laughed as we whipped past the ground and zoomed toward the sky again. "But it will make you tough. Don't you feel tougher already?" he shouted as our cage spun upside down again.

No, I did not feel tougher, and all I could do was continue to scream. Chase screamed too, only it was a scream of exhilaration. Then all I could think about was how I was stuck in a cage swooping a hundred feet in the air with a maniac who thought it was fun while I was sure I was going to die. I did learn one thing from the experience, and that was never again to listen to my brother, at least not to the point where I put my life in his hands.

When we finally got off and my feet were on the ground again, Chase held me by the shoulders while I tried to get my bearings. "There, now just think, you can tell your friends. I bet Jack hasn't been on the Zipper. I bet he's not as tough as you."

No, Jack had not been on the Zipper. But he also didn't have an older brother to force him into doing things when no one else was around. I never went on that ride again, but I have kept the ticket stub all these years.

If there has been one positive thing in my life over the past two years, it's that my bass playing has really improved.

During that first year Chase was a junkie, I'd drown out the squabbling between Mom and Dad by cranking up my amplifier. I'd practice for hours at a time. Jack had talked me into buying a secondhand bass. He was already playing with Bobby Yee and Steve Goertz off and on. They needed a bass player and they asked me to join the band.

We call ourselves The Pogos. We do a mixture of stuff, nothing much original, although Jack has come up with a few decent songs. So far, we've had only one gig and that was at a junior high dance. We are gearing up to play in the battle of the high school bands in August.

On the Saturday morning following Chase's arrest, Jack and I head to Griffin's Music where I am picking up my new Fender Precision bass. I'd bought it a month earlier and was having it adjusted.

"I hear Harris Reed got his hand broken," Jack tells me as we walk down the sidewalk. "Every knuckle in his hand was smashed."

"How did he do that?"

"He didn't do it. His dealers did. I guess he owed them and he couldn't pay."

I get a creepy feeling in my stomach. The image of messing someone up intentionally is like a scene from *The Sopranos*, not something that happens in my own neighborhood.

We pass a toy store where a small white unicorn in the window catches my eye. "I'll only be a minute. I'll meet up with you," I tell Jack.

He shrugs and continues toward the music store.

When I buy the toy I ask the clerk for a double bag so that you can't see through it. When I meet up with Jack again he asks me what I bought. "Something for Jade's little sister. It's her birthday."

I'm not all that good at lying, not like some people in my family. But Jack is busy inspecting another bass, much like the one I recently bought. "I think I like yours better," he says. "The vintage sunburst. It's more traditional."

The owner of the store appears with my new guitar. I lift it from the case and feel the weight in my hands, discovering all over again why I bought it in the first place. Jack and I had searched the music stores for months before I found this one. The first time I held it I couldn't believe how naturally it fit against me. When I played it, I was blown away by the tone. It was a little more than I wanted to pay, but it had everything I'd been looking for. Now I return it to the case, stuffing the bag from the toy store alongside it. I am on a high when we leave the store.

"I can't decide which guitar I want," Jack says. "I mean, once I've saved the money. But first I need a job that pays a lot more than ripping tickets at the theater," he moans. "I need one like yours." We stop at a cross-walk. The light turns green, but Jack is studying my guitar case. "Gordie, have you thought about keeping your bass locked up? I mean, it's worth a lot of money, and Chase has his bail hearing next week. What if he does come home?"

Man, I wish he hadn't brought that up. Not at that moment when I was feeling so good. But then, he doesn't know I installed a lock on my closet door months ago. That's where I keep my guitars. That's where I keep anything that can be sold for a few bucks. Jack doesn't know this because I've never told him. It's embarrassing to have to keep stuff locked up in your own house. "I'll look after it," I say.

THREE

Monday after school, the smell of a roast cooking and the warm scent of something freshly baked, brings me into the kitchen to see what's prompted Mom to cook after all these months.

"Hi, Gordie," she says, waving a spatula toward the cookies cooling on the counter. "Have a cookie. I have news. Your brother's coming home in a few days. He made bail."

I hesitate to take the cookie. It's not the news that I'm having trouble adjusting to, it's Mom being so cheerful. Dad is also in a lighter mood when he arrives home from work, although he is not as jubilant as Mom, so I suspect he is more cautious about the decision than she is.

As it turns out, once he's through detox, Chase will be coming home to live with us until his case goes to court. The judge at his bail hearing imposed a number of restrictions: He has to attend counseling, he has to abide by a curfew and he has to stay away from his druggie friends. I know it's this last one that makes Dad nervous. Things would never be where they are now if he'd had any control over Chase before.

At supper the talk between my parents turns to the practical side: how they are going to come up with the money. Fifty thousand dollars is what they need to bring Chase home. I nearly choke. Apparently bail has been set high because Chase is at high-risk for taking off.

They have no savings left; it's been spent on lawyer's fees and by Chase at various times when he stole their bank and credit cards. And then there were the times they'd bailed him out of drug debts so high he was threatened by dealers. They couldn't afford it, but they also couldn't let him get hurt.

The meaning of money has definitely changed for them. Two years ago it was a major decision to buy a five-hundred-dollar television set, and now they are talking fifty thousand dollars, and for what?

I really did wish they'd discuss their finances in private like they used to, before it required so much attention that it spilled over to when I was around. It's not a really comforting feeling knowing that your parents are totally broke.

"Well, there is also the s2000," Dad muses as he pushes the potatoes around on his plate.

I look up from my own plate in horror. Dad purposely avoids my gaze.

"Charlie Anderson has been wanting to buy it for some time. It would cut down on what we'd have to borrow against the house."

I know their finances are not my business, but since they insist on discussing them in front of me, there are some things I can't leave unprotested. "But you promised I could use it once I got my graduated license. I have that now."

"Look, Gordie, I'll buy another sports car someday. And when I do, you can help me pick it out. I'm really sorry, buddy. It's just that we could really use the money right now."

Mom is shaking her head. "It won't be necessary to sell the car. We'll take out a loan and return the money when this is all over."

"No." Dad's tone is abrupt. "Look, I'm borrowing as little money as possible. I don't want to be on the hook for fifty thousand dollars if something goes wrong."

By "something" he means if Chase takes off.

Jade is not at work that evening, and it's lonely without her. It seems the only times I feel good anymore are when I'm with her or when I'm playing with the band. I'd like to spend more time with her, but every time I think of asking her out, I picture some disaster happening with Chase. It's one thing to tell her about my brother. But she goes to a different school, and she's never met the real thing. I am paranoid that if I ask her out or if I have her over to the house, he'll show up, all spaced-out, demanding money, scaring her off. Right now, everything is so chaotic in my life it's better to keep things simple. At least that way, there will be no chance of her confusing me with him.

I spend the first hour at work sorting and hanging small packets of electronic parts from display hooks. It's a slow night, so it's a good time, my boss Ralph Barnes tells me, to teach me how to handle cash.

"I've had this store for thirty-five years, Gordie. For the first twenty-five, nobody was open on Sunday. But now I have no choice, if I want to compete. If I teach you to handle things, perhaps I can take the odd Sunday off. I'm too old to be working every day of the week."

Ralph is old, but he never tires of talking about his store. Once he's shown me how everything operates, I handle the transactions for the remaining hour. Before leaving the hardware store, I call Jade to find out what's going on. She's just brought her mother home from three days in the hospital. She had a very bad chest infection, although the way Jade relates it, it sounds as common as if she'd gone to the grocery store. "She's on mega doses of antibiotics and a heap of other drugs. She's sleeping right now. I could sure use a visitor if you're not doing anything."

It's raining again when I leave the hardware store. I walk uphill along the pavement, jumping rivulets, the smell of wet concrete filling my nose. The sound of car tires splashing through puddles prevents me from hearing the footsteps until they are right behind me. Suddenly, I am pushed hard against the wall. There are two of them, probably ten years older than me: teeth missing, pockmarked skin, greasy hair shining in the neon lights.

"Keep your mouth shut!" one of them orders, pinning my arms against the brick wall so I can't move.

The other waves a metal pipe in my face.

My heart is racing harder than it ever has and in a way I have never felt before. "What do you want?"

The guy with the pipe grins.

"Is this something to do with my brother?" I try to keep my voice steady, but I am not nearly as together as I try to sound.

"Bingo," announces the guy pinning me against the wall. He grabs my shirt collar, pulls me toward him, then pushes me back again, whacking me hard against the building, nearly knocking the wind out of me. "The creep owes us money. Two grand to be exact. He racked it up before he went and got himself arrested. Your brother has a bad habit of running up tabs. You'd better tell him from us that we want to get paid, or can we tell him ourselves? Are you expecting him home anytime soon?"

I shrug and lift my hands like I don't have a clue.

When the guy pinning me realizes I'm not going to run, he drops his hold on me. "You tell him he's got a week."

The guy wielding the pipe emphasizes the time limit by jabbing the pipe into my stomach. "A week. And if we don't get paid, he's going to be lying alongside his friend in intensive care."

I don't know what else to do but nod. All I want is to get away from there. The two of them start to walk away. The one who had choked me turns. "You tell your brother DC and Ratchet came calling."

I watch their backs for another minute, then I turn in the opposite direction and begin to walk fast. It isn't the way to Jade's place, but there's no way I'm about to go in the same direction as them. Feeling like I'm about to heave, I turn to the gutter. I break into a cold sweat. My mind is racing, and I don't remember how I even end up in front of Jade's apartment building. I stand there for several minutes trying to collect myself. It's not that I'm afraid of being beat up, although the thought of Harris and his smashed fingers doesn't help. It's more the idea that they'd been watching me that creeps me out. They know where I work. What else do they know about me?

Finally I make it up the stairs and to the door of Jade's apartment. She invites me in. I remove my wet shoes in the hall even though the carpet is threadbare.

Despite the distraction of almost being pounded out, it strikes me again how little her family owns. The exception is medical equipment and they own plenty of that: breathing apparatus of different types lies scattered about and bottles of prescription medicines are lined up next to the sink. The door to the bedroom where Mrs. Scott is sleeping is slightly ajar. Jade and her sister Holly share the foldout couch.

"Are you okay, Gordie?" she asks.

I realize that I'm shivering. "Oh, yeah. I'm just wet. It's really coming down."

"Hmm, well, sit down and let me make you some tea. And some toast. I'm sorry we don't have anything left from dinner. I've already made Holly a sandwich for lunch tomorrow with the leftover chicken."

I do my best to smile. "Tea is fine. I'm really not hungry." The truth is I'm not sure that I could keep anything down.

Jade is helping Holly make a piñata for a school project, running strips of newspaper through a lumpy paste, slapping them around a balloon. "It's going to be a peacock," Holly informs me as I sit in the chair across from her. "Jade got me a rainbow feather duster for the tail. Do you want to help?"

I sit at the table, trying to focus on sounding interested. It's hard to go from having my health threatened by a couple of hoods to the calm domestic scene in front of me without showing a little stress. I do manage to say, "I'm much better at model airplanes, but sure, I guess I can give it a try."

Holly sings quietly while we work. Jade starts the kettle boiling, a small television set murmurs in the corner, and despite the door being almost closed, Mrs. Scott's oxygen machine hums softly in the background. It's a new sound to me, but it eventually becomes part of the comfortable busy scene in the apartment.

Holly suddenly accuses me of not tearing my strips thin enough. "It's going to be all bumpy and not round."

I look at my work. She is absolutely right. The strips I've added are gargantuan lumps. I try to tear a thinner strip, but I'm still shaking so badly inside that I seem to have lost the ability to control my fingers. "I'll tell you what, I'm going to drink my tea and warm up before I do any more."

Jade sets the tea on the table before me.

Once the body of the peacock is finished, they balance it on a saucer to dry. Jade tells Holly to take a bath and get ready for bed. She promises they'll finish the neck and head the following day after school. "I'm sorry," she says when Holly is gone. "There's not much privacy around here. Maybe next time we can go out. It's just a little too soon to leave her alone." She motions toward the bedroom.

"It's no big deal," I tell her, glad for the moment that I don't have to go out.

And then I think of something, although I don't say it out loud. My family used to be something like this. Before the stealing and the lying, the threats and the thugs jumping me in the street, my family used to do normal things. They were interested in normal things. Things like hobbies and music lessons, not how they were going to come up with fifty thousand dollars to get one of us out of jail.

The following day, my first class isn't until ten thirty, so I drop by the hospital first thing in the morning. The redhead, Lisa, recognizes me. "Hi, Richard Cross's nephew," she says.

"Gordie," I remind her before I ask if there has been any change in Richard's condition.

She solemnly shakes her head. "He's still comatose. There's fluid on the brain that the doctors are trying to control. That's the biggest challenge right now."

Again I make sure he has no other visitors before I continue down the hall and enter his room. I pull the unicorn from my backpack and place it on the bedside table beneath the drawings. Three more have been added. They are not quite as colorful as the previous two. Nothing else seems to have changed since I'd first visited Richard Cross. He is still hooked to the machines and he does not appear to have even moved. I think of the CNN news commercial about how "nothing stays the same for a week, a day or an hour." It doesn't appear true in Richard Cross's case. His life was put on hold the moment Chase cracked him over the head. I feel like such a freak knowing what really connects me to him.

I think of Chase going through detox, sweating and puking, and I feel no sympathy for how he must feel. If anything, his misery leaves me numb. So, he'll live through it and he'll move forward; he'll recover. Richard Cross has shown no indication which way he'll go.

There is really nothing else for me to do, so I stay only a moment before going to school.

I have just collected my books for physics when Ms. Larson, the school counselor, stops me in the hall. "Gordie, do you have a minute after school?"

"What do you want to see me about?"

I realize that I am being watched by the two biggest tools in the school: Jason Dodds who is about five foot four with a mind and body about as agile as a barbecue, and Brian Zimmerman who is never without a two-liter bottle of Coke. When he grins, his teeth are all pitted and the color of a pumpkin.

Following my glance, Ms. Larson leans a little forward and lowers her voice. "I hear your brother's got himself into trouble. I just want to talk." Ms. Larson is young, enthusiastic and very professional. She is always dressed in suits with coordinating shoes. I try to imagine sitting across from her, telling her what it's been like living with Chase, the things he's done. I decide it wouldn't be much different than sitting down and spewing a string of obscenities in her face. "I'm sorry, I have to work," I lie.

Ms. Larson smiles before laying a hand on my shoulder. "Okay, well, anytime you want to talk, I'm always here."

I nod and continue down the hall. As I pass Jason Dodds, he flings open his locker and pulls out a lacrosse stick, nailing me in the gut.

"Geez, I'm sorry, Jessup," he sneers.

I grab the end of the stick and push it toward him.

"You'd better watch it," says Zimmerman. He's leaning against the locker next to Jason Dodds, swinging the bottle of Coke between two fingers. "I wouldn't turn my back on Jessup. He might smash you over the head."

Jason grins. I still hold one end of the stick. I want so badly to wrench it from his hands and take out a few of his teeth. But somewhere in the back of my head I know this would be stooping to his level, exactly what he wants. I relax my grip.

At the same moment Mr. Dublenko, my physics teacher, steps out of his classroom into the hallway. "Come on, fellas, get moving. The bell for the next class has already gone."

FOUR

Chase is home. At least I think they brought home the right guy. It has been six months since I last saw him, and I barely recognize the shriveled form they tell me is my brother. He is wearing the sports shirt and khakis pants I saw Mom leave the house with, folded across her arm. The shirt hangs on him like a flag on a flagpole in a dead calm. When I say hello to him, his eyes are vacant and his face is an expressionless wasteland. I'm can't even be sure he knows who I am. But then, for the past two years Chase has used meth as regularly as the rest of us have gone to bed at night and got up in the morning, and it shows.

For two days, Chase has been lying around the house like some invalid. Mom has taken two weeks off from her job as a secretary at an old folks' home. She says it's to help him put on weight, to help him get started on the road to recovery. But despite how she coddles him, he's not a helpless infant. He does know how to warm up a can of soup. No, I think it's more likely that she and Dad agreed she should take the time to prevent him from breaking his bail conditions. Although, when I see Chase walking down the hall without a shirt, I find it hard to believe that he'd have the strength to bend a straw let alone put a man the size of Richard Cross in the hospital.

On the third day he is home, Mom has to run some errands. When I get home from school, she tells me I am to look after Chase. "He's eaten well today," she says, like he's four years old and has just learned to tie his shoes. "He's watching a movie right now. Maybe you can start dinner, Gordie. Peel the potatoes and make the salad? I'll be back in time to cook the rest."

I have said little to Chase since he came home. It's hard to know what to say to him because, in a way, it's like some stranger is sharing the house. But the reality of what he's done has been sinking in, and Mom's approach that he should be pampered rather than held accountable is wearing thinner than his chest. Especially at four in the afternoon when I walk into the living room and see him sprawled on the chesterfield watching *Cape Fear* while I've been at school all day.

"Haven't you seen that?" I ask. "Like five times at least."

He holds a hand up to stifle me. "Shh, this is the best part."

I have told no one but Jack about Chase's dealers threatening me, and now, watching him lie there stuffing his face with taco chips and pistachios, the memory of Ratchet swinging that pipe sends me over the edge. I snatch the cushion from under his head and slam it over his face. Chase grabs my arms and struggles to get out from under it, but he has absolutely no grip. I am amazed at how totally weak he is. I pull the cushion off but continue to pin him down. "You whacked-out spineless creep! Your screwball dealers came looking for you. They beat on me instead. I don't want anything to do with you or your psycho friends. Do you hear me?"

"Get off of me," he splutters.

"They tell me you owe them two grand. How are you planning to pay that off? Mom's jewelry or Grandma's TV this time?"

Chase starts to whimper. "I don't know. But they broke Harris's hand. He owed them five hundred. They'll probably break my neck."

I stand up. I throw the pillow at him, but he has no reflexes, and it hits him square in the face. I realize why he hasn't attempted to leave the house. He's afraid of those two goons.

"Do you know Mom and Dad have risked the house on you? They've got no savings left. You've cost them everything they have."

"Yeah, I know," he says without emotion. "You've got to help me."

"Why should I? Look at you. There's a guy lying in the hospital with his head split open because of you, and you're still only thinking about yourself."

"I know. I'm sorry," Chase begins to snivel. "I didn't know what I was doing. Please, Gordie, if you can help me out this one time, I'll straighten out. I'll go back to school. Mom and Dad will keep the house, and it will all be okay."

It is a pitiful display. I am not swayed by his sniveling, and he's done way too much damage for things to ever be the same. But if his debt is paid, at least Mom and Dad won't have to deal with that on top of everything else. It's been more than annoying watching her cater to Chase, but in another way, it's also been a bit of a relief. She's been positive for a change. I've seen her lose it too many times over the past two years. But I don't have two grand. I have twelve hundred dollars in my bank account. I do still have a check from my grandparents in Ontario, money they'd sent to me for my birthday. And I get paid by Ralph Barnes later in the week.

I can't believe I'm even considering it. I pick him up by the neck of his T-shirt and drop him again. "If I do this, you'd better stay straight or I'll break your neck myself."

"I will." Chase immediately stops sniveling. It's amazing how quickly he turns the sobs off and on. "I promise. You'll see. I'll get a job. I'll pay you back."

I know Chase well enough to know that he is giving me his standard lines. But if I am doing this for anyone, it's for me and Mom and Dad. "All right, I'll think about it." I am not going to give him a definite yes. I want to make him grovel for a while.

Dad is letting me take the Honda s2000 to Bobby's house for a band practice. Bobby is the drummer in our band. He lives just below Cleveland Dam.

I have mixed feelings about driving the car. I can't wait to finally drive it, but Dad is only allowing it because he's selling it to pay off some debts. He admitted he wanted to give me a chance before it's gone. Jack and I set our guitars in the backseat and start in the direction of the Upper Levels Highway, headed toward Horseshoe Bay.

I am not used to how tight the gears are after driving Mom's old Toyota. It has great pick-up as we emerge onto the highway. I accelerate quickly, and we are soon flying past the Toyota's top speed. It has rained earlier in the day, so I am a little concerned about hydroplaning with a skiff of water still on the road. I hit 110 kmh and keep it steady.

"This is so cool!" Jack exclaims.

I agree. We have the windows down, the stereo on, and the damp spring air is, for the moment, helping me forget about home. I hope Dad hangs on to the car long enough so that I can take Jade for a drive.

We have just passed the Mountain Highway turnoff when a black Passat roars past us. It changes lanes directly in front of us before the driver throws on his brakes. I immediately slam on my own brakes—I miss plowing into him by millimeters.

Jack snaps forward like a whip. "What's that twit doing?"

The Passat continues slowly in front of us, forcing us almost to a crawl. A horn blares behind me. I glance at the reflection of the face of the woman in the car following me. She is fuming. In answer I pull into the left lane and roar ahead of the Passat. He follows, but he is soon tailgating me at 120 kilometers an hour. I can't believe what is happening.

"Did you do something?" Jack asks. He twists in his seat to get a glimpse of the nutjob following us. "Why is that guy so pissed off?"

"I don't know. He just came out of nowhere." Again I consult the rearview mirror. I switch lanes once again. He follows. I step on the accelerator, feeling the car become uneasy on the wet road. I am soon pushing 130 kmh—nervously.

"There are two guys in the car, about twenty-something," Jack tells me, "and they're laughing. What a couple of freaks."

And then it hits me—at 140 kilometers an hour. "Chase's dealers."

Jack's head swivels to the front. He looks at me in alarm. "What do they want with you?"

"They probably think I'm Chase. They must have heard he got out."

The Passat pulls into the lane next to us and comes alongside of me. I have just enough time to recognize Ratchet and DC before a siren suddenly sounds. It is so close it's like it has started up inside my head. In the rearview mirror, I spot the flash of the light on the roof of a police car coming up behind us.

"I don't believe this," Jack slides down in his seat. "The cops." The word comes out a little like a balloon losing its air.

As I begin to slow down to pull over, I am aware of the Passat taking off at lightning speed. The cops don't pursue them; instead, they follow me until I've come to a stop on the shoulder of the highway. Jack opens the door and starts to get out.

"Remain in your vehicle," orders an amplified voice.

Jack pulls his leg back into the car like he's been bit by a snake. He slams the door. "What should we do?"

"Stay in the car like they said."

"Why do they want us to do that?"

In the rearview mirror, I can see the two cops approaching the car. One is a graying, middle-aged guy, the other has a mustache and is younger by about ten years. They each have a hand on their holster. "Because they think we're criminals."

Jack groans as I roll down the window.

"Any idea how fast you were going?" the older cop who is on my side of the car asks.

"Some idea. Probably close to one twenty."

"Try one forty-seven," he replies. "Can I see your registration and license?"

I dig my license out of my wallet. "Don't go anywhere," he says, waving the license in the air. He takes both documents back to his car while the cop with the mustache remains next to the Honda. Jack and I sweat it out for ten minutes until he returns. He speaks to his partner before speaking to us. "Out of the car," he orders.

Jack and I get out. They have us put our hands on the roof of the car while they pat us down for weapons or drugs, I'm really not sure what. They then ask for the car keys, lock Dad's car and follow us back to their own vehicle where we are told to sit in the backseat. It turns out that Dad's car has seven outstanding parking violations. It also has been spotted in front of some well-known drug houses. Chase. Again. They are taking us to the police station to clear it up.

Jack and I both protest that we can't leave our guitars just lying out in the open in the backseat. The young guy looks at the old guy, who finally nods. At least we are able to convince him of this. We give up our jackets, and the younger cop returns to the Honda where he throws them across the backseat.

"I am sooo screwed," Jack whines on the drive to the station. He can't sit still. His knees are jiggling, and he cracks his knuckles like he always does when he gets nervous. "My parents will kill me when they hear how fast we were going. It's already like they're handing over the keys to Fort Knox when I ask them for the car."

I feel a little sorry for him. He has only one sibling, a sister who is not even ten. He's never experienced the repercussions of living with a criminal like Chase. Although I can't say many of my friends have.

Once we arrive at the police station, we are asked to wait in a small room with a wobbly table and three straight-back chairs. After a twenty-minute delay, the two cops who picked us up saunter back into the room.

"Okay." The older guy balances on the edge of the chair across from us. The other one stands behind him. "Let's try and get through this quickly. Why were you driving like you were in the Grand Prix?"

"We were being chased," Jack immediately offers.

"By who?" the cop questioning us asks, although somehow I get the feeling he already knows.

"No, we weren't." I knock Jack's knee under the table with my own. "I just wanted to see how fast the car would go. It was the first time my dad let me drive it."

The cop frowns. He seems a little annoyed that we aren't in agreement. Jack looks at me with raised eyebrows.

I attempt a small chuckle. "He just doesn't want me to get in trouble from my parents. Right, Jack? My Dad can be kind of tough when he wants to be."

Dad would certainly kill me, but I have no choice. I don't want him to know we were being hounded by Ratchet and DC. If they find out, I'll have to tell them about the money Chase owes. Thankfully, Jack clues in that something is up, and he doesn't say anything more.

The cops don't believe me, though. They saw the Passat take off. They had the license and they are fully aware of Ratchet and DC and their profession. The graying cop explains all this in a calm matter-of-fact voice, but in a way that also makes me feel like I'm just another lying kid who is stupid enough to think he's smarter than the cops. He says, "So, what we want to know is why they were chasing you. Are you dealers or users?"

It's almost funny the way Jack's mouth drops open. Although I do feel like a piece of scum just knowing that they would think we were either of those things. "Neither," I tell them. "I told you, I was trying out the car. I have no idea who was in that other car or why they were speeding."

"All right." The cop pulls a pen out of his shirt pocket and begins to fill out a form. It's a speeding ticket. I owe two hundred dollars. "You can go this time. But I'm going to warn you that you should be a little more careful who you go driving with. You're really lucky those guys didn't run you off the road."

Jack is allowed to go, but I have to wait for my parents to show up so Dad can deal with the parking tickets Chase has collected. Both Mom and Dad arrive with Chase in tow. One of them needs to drive Dad's car home and Chase, of course, can't be trusted to be left alone.

"Oh, Gordie," Mom says. A faint trail of mascara stains her cheek. She looks so disappointed in me, I feel like the worst heel on the face of the earth. "Imagine how we felt when the police phoned and told us you were here. Haven't we had enough to deal with without this?"

"I'm sorry," is all I can think of to say.

Dad speaks to the police officer at the front desk. He pays the fines. Mom drives home with Chase after she drops me and Dad off to collect the Honda. It's a miserable drive home, to say the least.

"What about trust, Gordie?" he says. "I thought that was at least something I could always count on with you. You broke that."

"Yes," I say, "I know. I just wanted to try it."

"But one hundred and forty seven?" he fumes. "What if you'd lost control? You would have been killed. You have no idea how that would have absolutely killed your mother and me."

I try to imagine what it would be like for them. They are already so fragile they probably would wither right up and blow away. "I'm sorry," I say again.

"Well, it's obvious I am doing the right thing. Selling it. This car is too much of a responsibility for you anyway."

FIVE

S teve and Bobby are a little ticked off that we didn't show up for the practice, until they find out why; then they are both impressed and amazed. We get together later that night at Jack's house to listen to music.

"You were clocked going one hundred and forty-seven!" Steve repeats when I tell him. "I got up to one hundred and thirty once. But one hundred and forty-seven, that would take a lot of nerve. Weren't you scared you'd wipe out?"

"I didn't have time to think about it. Those idiots were right on our tail."

Bobby is slumped back in an easy chair, spinning a drumstick. "What's it like being interrogated? Do the cops really put the screws to you the way they do on TV?"

"I don't know how other people are treated, but it wasn't as bad as all that," says Jack. He grimaces. "They weren't as tough as my dad was, that's for sure. I'm not allowed to drive his car for at least a month, and then it will be reviewed."

"But Gordie was driving," Steve points out.

"Yeah, which I told both my parents. They didn't seem to care. I was with him, so I must have been a part of it. I must have goaded him on or something."

"Sorry," I say.

"Ah, it's not you're fault. It's your doped-out brother's."

There is nothing to deny, and nobody disagrees.

"Hey, did they throw you in the tank?" Steve asks. "I mean, while you were waiting for your parents to get there. Did you have to share a cell with a load of thugs?"

"We were speeding." I drop a disc in the CD player. "We weren't suspected terrorists. Let's drop it, okay? I don't want to talk about it anymore." I press Play.

Chase doesn't say anything about what happened until I am alone with him the next day. "See why you've got to help me?" he gripes. "I told you—they'll kill me if they don't get paid."

Instead of apologizing for Jack and me almost being run off the road, for the police hassling me and Dad coming down on me, he makes it sound like it's a problem I brought on myself.

"You know what? This is *your* problem, not mine."

"Come on, Gordie. Just this one time, please? You know they don't fool around. If they don't kill me, they'll hurt me. Think what that would do to Mom."

"Don't you use that on me."

"Okay, okay. But I can't do anything until they're off my back."

"I'm still thinking about it."

Chase has been home for nearly two weeks. Payment to Ratchet is a week overdue. Mom and Dad are urging him to do something: enroll in school or apply for a job—anything. It will help build his confidence, they tell him. But more importantly, it will look good when his preliminary hearing comes up. That's the procedure used to decide if there's enough evidence to go to trial. I really don't know how much more evidence is needed, considering he'd been caught red-handed with the broken bottle in his hand and Richard Cross lying at his feet. But it could be months before the lawyers have all the paperwork figured out.

The one thing I do have to give Chase credit for is staying clean for two weeks. Even if it is the fear factor of being mutilated by his dealers, it's worked. But I'm also not naïve enough to believe it will continue. I've seen what has happened in the past and I've heard the statistics. A drug cop who spoke at school told us meth-amphetamine users have less than an eight-percent chance of recovering. Those are pretty poor odds for someone like Chase, who has no interest in cleaning up; even if he did, he has no perseverance. He's demonstrated that many times over the past year.

The first time Chase was picked up at a meth house and ordered to go to rehab, he was out in thirty days. When he came home he was right back at it within twelve hours. He'd told my parents he'd needed to borrow the car to pick up a few things.

"Like what?" Dad asked. There was no doubt by his tone that he didn't believe him.

But before he'd even had time to invent an excuse, Mom stepped in. She argued that they would eventually have to trust him again, so what was the harm in letting him take the car to the store. Reluctantly, Dad gave in.

Chase returned three days later; starving, stinking and ready to crash. Dad was furious. It was the first time I ever saw him blow up—I mean, really blow up. He was just hollering at Chase who was so amped-out he could barely keep his eyes open to listen to the rant. Dad did tell Chase that he would be out on the street if it happened again. A threat that I knew Mom would have difficulty letting him carry out.

As for Mom, she had gone nearly berserk in those three days. She'd driven around the seediest parts of the city, looking for him. She'd called all his old friends, not realizing they'd dumped him months before when he got into meth. The only response she did get was from Harris's mother, who hadn't seen her own son in weeks.

When he got home after his three-day binge, Chase slept for two days. Finally he got up, showered and, once he'd eaten everything in the fridge, asked Mom for fifty dollars. "What for?" Her tone was unusually demanding. "Why should I trust you this time?"

"It's for school," Chase persisted. "Look, Mom, I'm sorry I lost control. It was just a reaction to being cooped up in rehab for a month. But I know that I've got to change. Believe me, I am so thankful you guys have stuck by me through all of this. I don't know what would have happened to me if you hadn't. I need the money for the application fee for Outreach. If you want me to finish my diploma, I've got to apply."

Moms' face softened. If Chase could get a diploma for being a manipulator he would have graduated a long time ago. She gave him the money along with a warning that she really should call the college and run it by Dad, but she didn't want to interrupt his teaching, so she wouldn't as long as Chase gave her his personal promise that he wouldn't take off.

He didn't take off, but he did come home at midnight, high. Mom and Dad were in bed, although it wasn't likely they'd been asleep. Chase had phoned around eight to say he was going to a movie. Still, not until they heard him come through the door could they ever really relax.

"Say, what's up, Gordie?" Chase was flying. He plunked down on the end of my bed, grabbed a pen from my desk and began following the pattern on my comforter, over and over.

"Did you apply?"

"Huh?"

"To go back to school."

Chase laughed. "Oh, yeah, I applied to the school of life. That's where I'm going. I'm thinking of sales. I think I could make a killing at it. You ever notice how I can talk anybody into anything? I'm a natural. With my looks and personality, nobody turns me down."

His ego made me gag. Sitting there at the end of my bed, looking like he just rose from the dead, and he's telling me how good looking and intelligent he is. "Have you looked in the mirror lately? A cadaver would have a better chance of selling a car than you."

He didn't say anything; he was totally fascinated by the pen. I knew he could go on geeking like that for hours. If I left him until noon, he'd still be sitting there tracing the pattern with the pen.

"You're an ass," I told him. "Get out of my room."

Over the next three months, Chase came and went, lying about where he was going and where he'd been.

Stuff started disappearing from the house: small electronics and jewelry, Dad's watches. At first, Chase denied taking these things. He'd turn the conversation around, trying to place the blame on us for misplacing them. He'd get so worked up denying it that we'd drop it. It got to the point that not a word that came out of his mouth was believable or made any sense. Then, one night he was caught stealing a DVD player from a car at the neighborhood shopping center. He was fined, given a conditional sentence and sent back to rehab again.

When he got out a month later, Dad arranged for Chase to stock shelves in a small grocery store. Mr. Pelltiere, a longtime friend of Dad's, managed the store and he agreed to do Dad the favor. Chase blew it within two weeks. Ryan and Harris started hanging around. The stuff Chase was supposed to be shelving went missing. Customers complained about the weird behavior and strange appearance of the stock boy in aisle eight.

Life became a nightmare for all of us after that. Chase came and went as he pleased. Dad would confront him when he could pin him down. He'd lay it all out: Chase had to get work or he was out of the house. He couldn't keep taking advantage, using the house to shower and eat when he crashed and finally couldn't stand his own stink. Chase would sit there, nodding in agreement that yes, he was wasting his life, blowing every chance he got and that he'd better shape up. But he didn't hear any of it. He didn't hear them and he sure didn't listen to me.

But experience had taught me that there was nothing to be gained in trying to reason with a drug addict, whether he's high or craving the next hit, which were the only times I ever saw him. Not that I didn't try. But I could think of no other way to make him listen. We were only a year apart in age, but we were so very different. When it came right down to it, we'd had little in common since we were too small to be left on our own, when we were jointly referred to as "the boys."

Chase lost fifty pounds off his five-foot-ten-inch frame. He broke out in "speed bumps"—sores that oozed gross stuff as his body tried to get rid of the noxious chemicals. He'd scratch and pick at them even as you talked to him, never allowing them to heal. One of his bottom teeth came loose and fell out—he didn't seem to notice. Mom and Dad argued day and night, and I was sure they were ready to split up.

Then, six months before the assault on Richard Cross, we got a call from Grandma, Dad's mother, in the middle of the night. Chase was marching through her house waving a knife, strung out, demanding money. She had none in the house. Dad jumped in the car while I kept her on the phone.

Grandma was scared and confused. "Gordie," she said, "what's happened to him? I've never seen anybody act like this."

It was all I could do not to drive over and punch Chase out. I spent the next ten minutes trying to convince her that it had nothing to do with her, or any of us. She should know that, she was a nurse. This is what drug addicts do: they demand, they bully, they take.

"Yes," she said, crying.

"What's he doing now, Grandma?"

"I can't see him. I'm in the bedroom."

I pictured Grandma huddled in her room, alone in the house with Chase. It was an image so not like her. She was normally tough and independent. She'd carried on working at a clinic another ten years after Grandpa had died suddenly, managing the house and huge garden and still insisting on cooking all the holiday dinners herself.

"I think he's going through the kitchen drawers. What's he looking for?"

"Something he can sell. Just let him. Stay where you are, Grandma. But if he does come in there demanding something, give him your old TV—the one in the storage room."

"But it doesn't work."

"He doesn't know that. Just let him take it. Dad will be there right away."

"Oh, Gordie. I'm so frightened for him. Oh, thank goodness," she sighed with relief, "your Dad is here."

I hung up when the dial tone sounded.

When Chase saw Dad's car, he took off out the back door. Dad brought Grandma home to stay with us that night. The whole thing of Chase showing up, drugged out and demanding money, scared her so much she put her house up for sale within a week. Not just because of Chase, she insisted, but because of rising crime in the city in general.

We didn't see Chase again for two weeks. Dad had already emptied his room and moved all his stuff to the garage when he showed up like nothing had happened. He wandered into the front hall on a Sunday morning.

"What are you doing here?" Dad demanded.

"I'm hungry," he said. "I need a place to sleep."

"Well, you're not doing it here. You can collect your things, they're in the garage. You're not coming back here, Chase."

It was a really tough thing for Dad to do. Mom had gone into her bedroom, where she was crying. Through all their arguing, they'd agreed it was the only way he might come around. Maybe they were just encouraging his habit by giving him a place to stay. Maybe if they let him really hit bottom it would make him realize what he'd become and he'd ask for help.

Dad allowed Mom to make Chase a sandwich; then he watched him put a few things in a backpack before he left. It was a harsh moment. For Mom and Dad, I knew it was probably beyond their imagination that after years of school and family holidays, Christmases, soccer games and birthdays, this was the way one of their children would leave home.

A few days later, Chase entered the house when no one was home and stole Dad's camera. My parents became paranoid about going anywhere, in case Chase broke in again. He continued to show up a couple of times a week wanting money. For groceries, he told Mom. He was so withered and gaunt she couldn't help herself. Chase would leave with sixty or seventy dollars, and always, the empty promise that he would clean up. Because Chase often showed up in the middle of the night, Mom began leaving money under the doormat so he wouldn't wake up Dad.

Chase had become a huge financial drain. I asked Mom why she kept giving him money. She knew where it was going.

"He's my son, Gordie. I don't know what else to do. I hope at least some of it goes to feed him."

Three times she gave him the first month's rent on a bachelor apartment. Three times it went up his nose. One morning we got a call from the hospital. Chase had blacked out in a parking lot, fallen down and hit his head. Someone had called the police, and he was now in the psychiatric ward at the hospital. But by the time Mom and Dad got there he had walked.

He showed up at the nursing home where Mom worked, scaring the pants off the old folks. He embarrassed Dad by wandering into a class he was teaching. He stood at the back of the room, his bug eyes staring blankly, his spastic movements distracting everyone until Dad excused himself. He took him out in the hall, gave him fifty dollars and told him never to show up at his work again. It didn't stop him, because all that ever mattered to Chase was that he got his next fix.

Less than a month before Chase knocked Richard Cross on the head, I came home from school to find Mom sitting at the kitchen table puzzling over the statement from a credit card she'd never owned. The bill was for five thousand dollars—the card was maxed out. The invoice included motel rooms, taxi rides, some groceries, but mostly cash withdrawals—a couple of hundred dollars at a time. Chase had applied for the card in Mom's name, using documents and bank receipts he had found around the house.

Mom and Dad were stunned at the amount of money they owed and the depth of Chase's betrayal. Most amazing to me was that Chase still possessed the mental faculties to sneak into the house and put something like that together. After that, Dad had the locks changed.

A few days later, Mom locked herself in the washroom where she wouldn't have to hear Chase on the other side of the front door, his key useless, mumbling that he was hungry and had nowhere to go.

But even when he was out of the house, Chase never left my parents' minds. All their energy went into thinking about him, why he was the way he was, and how they could get him to change.

I didn't know how to deal with it anymore. I was angry at them for falling for all his lies. And yes, I was angry at them for ignoring me and anything I did, in favor of catering to the self-centered whims of a meth head. But it was watching the emotional roller coaster he had them on that was the worst. The possibility that he might stick it out after rehab—actually do something with his life—followed by the inevitable letdown the first time he showed up stoned. I didn't know how many highs and lows they could take before they also dissolved.

arris is dead. I hear the news through Jack. Harris died of twenty-seven stab wounds to his legs and chest. When I hear the news, I immediately think he must have been murdered as punishment for not paying his drug debts. But that isn't what happened. The wounds were self-inflicted. Harris was alone in a park after leaving some friends. They said he was tweaking, strung out so bad he was making no sense and hallucinating to the point that he was freaking them all out. He couldn't get rid of the crank bugs crawling all over his skin. Sitting on the grass beneath a streetlamp, Harris attacked them with a penknife, over and over. He'd lost a lot of blood before he was found by a jogger early the next morning; he died before they got him to the hospital.

Chase registers little surprise when I tell him. He may have already known, although I doubt it. He reacts to news of Harris's death with the same generic look of distant comprehension that he reacts to any news these days.

I could have told him the toilet was overflowing for all the emotion he shows. But then, I don't think he truly understands much anymore, not fully. It seems to take him forever to process even the simplest conversation. I really don't know how he can stand it—I'd be scared to death if my brain wasn't working anymore.

On the other hand, he probably didn't have a real deep friendship with Harris. People who become friends because they are both into drugs can't have a whole lot more in common. If they did, if they had real interests or hobbies, they wouldn't be using. But what do I know? It just seems a pretty exclusive club for freaks.

"Thank god, you're not into that stuff anymore," Mom says, probably hoping it will help convince Chase that he isn't.

Dad is a little more forthright. "That could have been you, Chase."

"I don't get how you could stab yourself even once," Jack says on the way home from school. "I mean, intentionally. Okay, maybe once if you're goofing around and it's an accident. But twenty-seven times makes no sense."

Jack is understandably confused by the whole thing. I, on the other hand, am shocked but I do sort of comprehend. "Think of it as a meltdown. You fill your brain with a toxic mixture of chemicals and crap, and over time, everything starts to short-circuit."

"Yeah, I guess. But twenty-seven times? He was truly fried."

Over the next few days, Chase becomes more and more restless. Whether this has anything to do with Harris's death, I'm not certain. I do know it is long past Ratchet's due date for repayment of his loan. I am leaving for work a few days later when he pulls me aside. "Gordie, can you lend me five hundred? Just five hundred."

Just five hundred. He says it like I can pull it out of my pocket. Like five hundred dollars is loose change. Still, I wonder why he doesn't ask for what he owes. "Why five hundred? I thought you owed two thousand."

"I do. But if I pay some of what I owe to Ratchet at least I can leave the house. I'll tell him the rest is coming."

"No way." I bend down to pull on my shoes. "When I have it, you'll pay the whole thing off at once. And I'm going with you. Don't think I'll just hand you two thousand dollars and watch you walk out the door. I might as well throw it into a strong wind off the Lion's Gate Bridge."

I step onto the bus. As the doors wheeze shut behind me, I make my way to the back where no one can watch me think. I have to figure out how I can get rid of Chase's debt and get him out of the house and working. It has become crucial, because something else has happened.

Mom has lost her job. They told her at the nursing home that it was because they no longer needed three people in the office. It was more likely because she kept asking for time off. From their point of view, I guess Mom has become about as dependable as Chase.

Mom is trying to remain positive; she says it couldn't have come at a better time. She means considering how she is needed at home. But with the debts Chase has built up, the lawyer's fees, and the house mortgaged for bail money, I know how much they depend on her income. While the bus fills up, I decide I will sell my old Yamaha. I could have traded it in for three hundred dollars when I bought my new bass, but at that time, I'd wanted to keep it. I'm not sure why. I almost never play it now. I guess it was more because it sort of got me started with the band. But now I wonder why I'm hanging on to it. If you get too sentimental about stuff you only end up getting hurt when you eventually lose it. Besides, it wasn't that good to begin with, and I bought it secondhand. With that, the check from my grandparents and what I have in the bank, I can pay Chase's debt. Maybe then he can join the real world and contribute for a change.

Jade is supposed to be at work, but she is already more than an hour late. I am hoping to grab a minute alone with her—I want to run my plan of paying off Chase's debt by her. I can't tell Jack. I already know what he'd say. He'd say I'm nuts and that there is no way he'd do it. He'd then quote all the times Chase has ripped me off. I would say the same thing if I was in his position. Jade is more likely to see it from my point of view: to take into consideration the need to get Chase out of the house and doing something, and to do it without Mom and Dad finding out.

It's a Thursday night and the store is busy with people picking up what they need for weekend projects. Admittedly it's not rocket science, but I have become very quick on cash. Ralph prefers me to handle it when there are lineups. He says his patience is wearing too thin to deal with peoples' tempers. They are always in such a hurry, and they don't like to wait for an old man fumbling around. The lineup is five people deep when the phone rings. Ralph is in the storeroom. I answer it at the same time as I continue to work the till.

"Gordie, I need money."

My stomach clenches at the sound of Chase's voice. Where does he get the nerve to call me at work? "Not now, Chase. I'm busy."

"But it's important."

"It's always important. Does it ever occur to you that what I'm doing might also be important?" I cringe a little. I sound exactly like my dad.

The lady I am taking money from raises an eyebrow before shifting her attention to the lightbulbs I am stuffing in a bag.

"Just two hundred. That'll do it for now."

"This morning it was five hundred. What is this for, Chase?" For the sake of the customers, and only the customers, I try to keep my rising anger in check. "Something tells me you're not going to use it to pay off your debt."

"Of course I am. Do you think I want Ratchet coming after me the way he went after you?"

I feel my cheeks burn. But there is no point in correcting him—Chase is so out of touch with reality, he probably really does think that Ratchet was after me for something *I* had done. I scan the next customer's items. "Later, Chase."

"It's for a down payment."

"Later." I hang up. I try to smile at the next person in line. It isn't very natural, though, and I probably just look like a guy who is suffering from gas.

The phone rings again.

"Busy place," the customer says.

I shrug in apology before glancing at the call display. It's my home phone number again. I ignore it. It rings eight times before Ralph, all red and sweaty from moving boxes, emerges from the storeroom.

"Aren't you going to answer that?" He pushes a shock of gray hair aside, leaving a smudge of dirt across his forehead.

"It's a wrong number."

"How do you know?"

"The same guy phoned a few minutes ago."

Ralph cocks his head a little as the phone continues to ring. I hate lying to him. Ralph always answers his phone, he listens to his customers, and that's how he's run his business for thirty-five years. The man in line takes the bag I hand him and leaves. Ralph returns to the storeroom. Chase doesn't give up until the twentieth ring and I am ready to reach through the phone and wring his scrawny neck.

Traffic in the store has slowed down when the phone rings half an hour later. This time, it's Jade calling from the hospital. She had taken her mother to emergency that morning. Her lungs had become filled with fluid, and Jade was unable to help her. She sounds shaken and a little uncertain, not her usual positive self.

"You go." Ralph waves toward the door when I tell him. "It sounds like she could use a little support. I'm fine. The rush is over."

Jade is waiting for me in the front lobby of the hospital. Holly is asleep with her head in Jade's lap. Jade looks tired and drained, like she has barely enough energy to get up from the row of chairs. She gently moves Holly aside and gets to her feet. "I'm so glad you're here," she says.

It's instinctual to hug her. It seems to be what she needs most right then. Besides, I can't think of anything to say. I can't tell her it will get better because I know that with her mother's disease that won't happen. So I hold on to her until I think I feel her gain a little strength. But then she begins to really cry. I pull her closer.

"I'm sorry," she says. "It's just...well, I don't know how much more of this I can take. I'm supposed to be at work. I'm supposed to be studying for an exam. I had to tell my friend Laura that I couldn't go to the mall to see the sweater she said would look perfect on me. I never have even two seconds to myself." Wiping her cheeks with the palms of her hands, she backs away a little. "I know all that sounds so selfish."

"No, it doesn't," I tell her. "It sounds normal."

Jade takes another moment to collect herself. "They're going to try some new antibiotics. The ones she's been taking don't seem to be doing much good anymore. The doctors want to keep her for a few days to see how it goes."

"Are you ready to go home?"

She nods. "Can you wait with Holly while I make sure there's nothing else she wants?"

"Of course." I sit down next to Holly on the row of chairs. Holly's small body rises and falls in sleep. I'm amazed that she can sleep at all under the bright lights and with the door opening and closing, but I guess she's probably used to being shuffled around. I pick up a six-month-old copy of *Sports Illustrated* from the table and open it up. People have been coming and going since I arrived, and I'm not sure why I look up when I do.

I spot a woman of about thirty with a small girl in tow moving quickly through the lobby, on her way out of the building. The woman is thin and tall, and wears her blond hair pulled back in a hairclip. Her face is strained and her lips are set. She marches toward the door in a determined way, a way that makes me think that she won't tolerate any interference.

The little girl has to run to keep up with her. Her long sandy hair is tangled like it hasn't been combed in days. I notice that particularly because it doesn't somehow fit with the trendy denim skirt and jacket she wears, although she does wear two different-colored socks. She holds tightly to the woman with one hand; with the other, she hugs a small unicorn against her chest. She is trotting along so quickly that she stumbles. The unicorn goes flying from her hand and skids across the polished floor. "Mom, my unicorn!"

I am close enough that I reach it before her mother realizes what has happened. I hold it out to her.

"Oh," says her mother, stopping. "Hannah, say thank you to the young man."

Hannah smiles shyly. She wraps an arm around the toy and takes it from me. I try to smile back, but it's all I can do not to blurt out my story, to tell them how very sorry I am, and that if it were in my power, I would do anything to turn things back.

"Come, Hannah."

I look after them.

"What is it?" Jade has returned. She takes the magazine from my hands and sets it on the table.

"That woman who just left, that was Richard Cross's wife, with their kid."

Jade turns to look, but she is too late. "Oh, I'm sorry, Gordie."

I call a cab. I ride home with Jade and Holly. On the way, I can't shake the image of Richard Cross's wife and his little girl sitting across from the comatose man. Do they talk to him as he lies there with the machines pumping? Do they tell him what they've done that day? Do they fill him in on all the things that have happened since Chase hit him on the head? I am so preoccupied by these thoughts that it is not until after we have dropped Jade and Holly off at their apartment and I have instructed the cab driver to take me home that I realize I have forgotten to tell Jade about my plan to pay off Chase's debt.

I pay the driver and get out of the cab. I am walking up our front walk when Chase's druggie friend, Ryan, appears from out of the shadows on the other side of the street. He walks toward me.

"Hey, Gordie." His tone is humble.

"What are you doing here?" I study his eyes in the dark. They are pretty dull, but I can't be sure he is wasted.

"I came to talk to Chase, but your parents won't let me see him."

"And you're surprised? They paid fifty grand to get him home. Do you really think they want to risk losing it all by having him hang out with you?"

He wipes his nose with the back of his hand—a druggie habit. Still, he looks down at his feet in a way that makes me thinks he isn't high. He shows no trace of that plastic confidence I am used to seeing in Chase. He looks back at me, and this time, I know he is talking sober. "It's not like that. You heard about Harris?"

"Yeah, I did. That was a pretty nasty way to end up."

Ryan nods. "I'm scared. I don't want that to happen to me. I'm going to check into rehab, and I'm going to stay there as long as it takes."

"Yeah?"

"Yeah. I came to talk Chase into coming with me. That's why I wanted to see him, but your dad closed the door as soon as he saw me."

"Huh, well, even if you'd told Dad why you'd come, he would have done the same thing. Why should he believe you? You guys can't discuss the weather without lying about it."

Ryan drops his eyes again. "Yeah, I guess."

"Anyway, he won't go," I tell him. "Not because you've decided to go."

"Will you ask him?"

I shrug. "Yeah, sure. I'll ask him. But don't wait for him. If you're serious, go check yourself in."

Ryan backs up a little. "Yeah, okay." He turns and starts down the sidewalk.

I don't believe that he will do it. Harris's death has shaken him up, there's no doubt about that. But I figure he'll be wasted by the end of the night and by morning, he'll have convinced himself that Harris had somehow brought it on himself. He'll continue to use as though he's invincible.

Still, it can't hurt to say it. "Good luck, Ryan."

He waves.

SEVEN

Three days later, I sell my old Yamaha, cash my checks and withdraw all my savings. I walk home with two thousand dollars in my pocket. I have never had so much money on me or even seen it all at once. It's five in the afternoon and despite the bank being only six blocks from my house, I have never been so jumpy. Even the shadow of a seagull passing over my head makes my heart leap to my throat. Every time a car slows I stash my hands in my pockets and pick up my pace. I desperately hope that it isn't those two losers who are going to wind up with my cash anyway.

In the end, I haven't discussed what I'm about to do with anyone. I really don't see any other way out. Mom and Dad are already so financially strapped, and Grandma would make me promise that I wouldn't do it. She'd tell me she would find the money herself. That would be a real hardship on her fixed income, and Jade...well, she has problems of her own.

So I've decided it's best to get it over with and get on with life in our house. I still have my job—I'll work extra shifts to cover the check my grandparents sent me. But I do plan on getting my money back from Chase eventually, even if I have to stoop to Ratchet's level and extract it with a little blood.

My parents are pleased that we're going to a movie together. At least that's what I told them Chase and I are doing when I asked to borrow Mom's car. I know she's hoping that we've found something in common to bring us closer together. I hate lying to her, but I can hardly tell her that fending off Chase's drug dealers is the reason we're going out.

I back out of the garage and sit in the car in the driveway, waiting for Chase. When he finally slides into the front seat, he immediately flips down the mirror on the visor. He pats his hair in case, between the house and driveway, a strand or two has fallen out of place.

Chase reeks of some heavy sweet cologne and he is wearing a new shirt. It reminds me of how he used to clean up after a five-day bender when he was ready to head back out on the street. I back out of the driveway. "I don't know why you got all dressed up to visit a couple of thugs. Do you think if you look good they won't hold a grudge? Keep in mind this is the last time you're going to see them."

Chase doesn't say anything. He just sits, staring straight ahead.

"Ever."

"What?"

"You're not going to see or contact them after tonight. And once you get a job you're going to pay me back, two thousand plus interest. Then we'll talk about the stuff you stole."

I just assume we are headed for the Eastside, the sleazy part of town where the smell of garbage and urine-soaked concrete drifts from the alleys and where those who gather have only one thing on their minds. But the Eastside isn't where Chase directs me. Instead, once we've crossed the Second Narrows Bridge, I follow his directions until we are driving down an older street in Burnaby. This is a family neighborhood; bicycles lie in the driveways and potted plants decorate the front steps.

"Stop here." Chase motions just ahead, to a house on the left.

I pull to the side of the road, across from the gray stucco bungalow he's pointed out. There are two cars parked in the carport, a third on the driveway and two on the street in front. The Passat that had hounded Jack and me on the Upper Levels Highway is one of them.

"This is it? This is where you come to get high?"

Chase appears nervous. He pats his hair again. "Yeah."

"But there are bicycles in the driveways and a stroller across the street."

"Yeah, so?"

"You are such a scuzz."

Chase holds out a hand. At first I'm not sure what for until I realize it's for the money.

"Oh, no. I'm going with you." I flip the door handle and start to get out.

"No." Chase's reply is almost a shout. "You can't."

I look at him.

"I mean, it's not a good idea. They won't let me in if they see you. They won't trust you. I'll just go in and pay them. You can watch me from here."

I close the door again. "I don't trust *you*."

"I'll be five minutes. You'll be sitting right here. I'm not kidding, they'll slam the door in my face if you're with me. We'll be out of here faster if you just wait."

I know he's about as trustworthy as a rabid skunk. But he is within my sight, and I guess I figure he won't try anything with me right here.

"All right, you've got five minutes. If you're any longer, I'll be pounding on that door until it comes down." I dig the envelope containing the two thousand dollars out of my pocket. "This is it, Chase. Your last chance. Pay those losers off, get back here and leave this crap behind you."

Chase nods. He snatches the money from my hand, removes it from the envelope and rolls it into a wad.

He stuffs the roll in his pocket, letting the envelope fall to the floor of the car. He is twitchy. I figure he's nervous about facing his dealers. I watch as he crosses the scruffy yard and knocks on the front door. He turns and looks at me once, but he doesn't acknowledge me. I glance at the clock. Six minutes after ten. The door opens and he disappears inside.

I wait. It's now quite dark and Burnaby Mountain looms close. A car drives by and turns into the driveway of the house two doors down on the same side of the street. A man steps out from the driver's side. He holds the back door for two young children while they jump out. All the time he stares at me sitting in Mom's car in front of the drug house. It creeps me out that if he knows what goes on inside his neighbor's house—and how could he not know with guys like Chase and Ratchet coming and going at all hours—he probably thinks I'm a druggie.

The blinds are drawn in the two windows that face the street. The small front yard is neglected: weeds grow through the bark mulch, which looks like it was thrown down at some attempt to landscape many years back. A dead cedar stands in the corner of the yard next to the driveway. Red needles lie scattered around its base.

I look at the clock again. Ten minutes after ten. It has been four minutes since Chase walked through the door. God, I hope this changes things. Chase still has to face the assault charges, but if he's working and Mom and Dad can return to dealing with the regular hassles of life—the fridge on the fritz or repairing a burned-out headlight—life would be so unbelievably good.

A car pulls up behind me. Two guys and a girl get out. The girl I notice the most: stringy hair, legs like bowed matchsticks, stumbling behind the two guys like an awkward starving goat. When the door opens, they immediately enter the house.

Ten fifteen. Nearly ten minutes. Okay, I'll cut him some slack. He may not have found those two right away, or they may have been busy. I have no idea how their business works. I begin to worry about sitting outside the house, waiting for a guy who's both a criminal and a user. What if the cops pick that night to raid the place? They know who owns the Passat and what they do for a living—I'd learned that at the police station. They have to be aware of what goes on inside the house and occasionally they must clean it out. Wouldn't that be just great? Me, not only arrested for frequenting a meth house but responsible for helping Chase break bail.

Ten twenty. My pocket feels empty. The money had been noticeable, clumsy at first, but after carrying it around for several hours, I certainly notice it's gone. Ten twenty-one. I am starting to worry. What if he doesn't come out? I want to go in and haul him out about as much as I want to eat a bowl of mud. I told him he had five minutes. It has been fifteen. Just five more. Surely he will be back by then. And if not, well, I don't have much choice but to go in after him, although he's sure going to hear about making me sweat.

The door opens. The two guys who parked behind me return to their car without the girl. They take off. Maybe Chase is having trouble getting out. Maybe his dealers decided to beat him up a little for interest on the two thousand. Whatever the reason, he is still in there, and I've waited long enough. As I open the car door my heart begins to race. It's not knowing what to expect that frightens me. On the other hand, I don't have to actually go into the place. All they have to do is hurry Chase up and send him out.

I follow the crumbling concrete sidewalk leading to the front door and lift the knocker. Moments later the door is opened by a man whose age is hard to judge. The whites of his eyes are the color of egg yolk, and he is thin, except around the middle where his liver bulges. He stands next to the door guardedly, and he doesn't relax when he finds someone unfamiliar standing on the other side.

"I'm looking for Chase."

The guy scratches the lose skin of his throat. The entire back of his hand is scarred—like the skin has been ripped off or it has been horribly burnt. "He's not here."

For a moment, his answer stumps me. I know Chase is in there. Maybe he just hasn't seen him. "But he just went in. I watched him walk through the door fifteen minutes ago."

"I didn't say he wasn't here. I said he's not here now."

Okay, I'd been watching the door the entire time. The guy is mistaken. "He must be. I would have seen him leave."

He shrugs. "I'm telling you, he's not." He begins to close the door. I thrust my foot between the door and the jamb to prevent it from closing.

"I'd like to take a look myself. I'm his brother. All I want is to find him and take him home."

This time, the man scrutinizes me more closely. Perhaps he believes me, but more likely he knows I'm a lot stronger than he is, and I'm not going to give up. Besides, judging by the cars in the driveway, he probably has plenty of backup inside the house.

"All right," he says. "Suit yourself." He wanders away, leaving me to step inside and find Chase myself.

It is a filthy house, made worse by the peeling wallpaper and the dingy light. There is no furniture in the tiny living room, just an old sleeping bag on the floor with a couple of bodies lying across it. They don't move. Their unnatural positions tell me they aren't sleeping, but passed out. Clothes and blankets, dirty and threadbare, lie in piles around what should be a dining room. A couple sit on the floor across from one another, sharing a pipe. They don't acknowledge me.

I cross the floor, following the man who answered the door to a room at the back of the house. It's the kitchen, although it doesn't look like much cooking or eating goes on. The cabinets are beat-up and hang off their hinges, there is no stove and the refrigerator door is missing. Ratchet, DC and some other loser sit at the table, smoking weed. The thin man who answered the door leans against the wall.

"Well, look who's here," Ratchet announces.

"Where is he?" I ask.

Ratchet's expression immediately changes. It occurs to me that he probably thinks that I'm here to buy— brought here by Chase.

"Where's who?" DC asks.

"You know who—Chase. He just paid you two thousand dollars."

Ratchet and DC look at each other. The look makes me sick. I instantly know that this isn't what happened. "I gave him two thousand. He was going to pay off his debt."

DC stands up. "Five hundred," he says. "He gave us five hundred. He said he's come into a pile of cash and he'll bring more tomorrow. It's all he could withdraw at once."

I stare at them. I can't believe what is happening, yet I do believe it. I think I'd been expecting it. I'd never really believed him. It was only hope that made me do what I did. I feel like screaming, beating them until they tell me it's a lie and Chase really had paid the full amount. "Where is he?" I manage to repeat.

Ratchet motions toward the door leading off the kitchen into the backyard and shrugs. "He left. We gave him a little incentive to ensure he comes back tomorrow. Hey, it's the first time he's come up with so much cash at once. We took it."

It's all I can do not to lunge at him. He could be lying. I tear out of the room and down the hall. I open a bedroom door and flick on the light. Three people lie on a bare mattress on the floor. They are so out of it, I could have been a SWAT team and they wouldn't have reacted. I recognize one of them as the skinny girl I'd seen arrive with the two guys that have since left, but there is no Chase.

I slam the door and look in another room across the hall. There is one guy, sitting on the floor, in a room empty of furniture. He is chipping at the floor with a pair of pliers. When he looks up, I get the feeling he's about to sling the pliers at me, so I close the door again.

The bathroom is a rathole, but it's empty. I find the basement door off the hall and pound down the wooden steps. The last riser is broken, and I stumble before hitting the concrete floor. It is a slum: one open space filled with half a dozen people stoned out of their heads. But Chase is not among them. I return to where Ratchet and DC still sit. By now, I am in a total panic. "He's not here."

DC crushes his cigarette butt in a jar lid. "That's what we told you. He left."

He couldn't have gone far the way he'd been itching to get cranked up after more than a month. I bolt into the backyard. It's nothing more than a patch of weeds and stubble stretching to a small wooden shed at the back. There is no patio or garden, only a few broken lawn chairs. The entire property is surrounded by a low, chain-link fence.

I check inside the shed. I feel around until I find a pull-chain for an overhead light. Illuminated by one bare bulb I survey the clutter of boxes, broken glass and needles littering the wood plank floor. There is no Chase. The yard backs directly onto the neighbors' properties in three directions. There is no alley. Chase would have had to hop the fence to take off, but I have no way of knowing in which direction and it's now very dark. I choose the neighbor's yard to the east, the one with the easiest access. Searching between the hydrangeas and rhododendrons, I back into a swing, which creaks and starts a dog barking. A light goes on in the house. I sprint around to the front and return to Mom's car.

I clench my fists and beat them against my legs. Hysterical. I've only read the word in books and heard it referred to in movies, but I know this is what it must be like. It's like I've gone deaf and blind all at once. I can't think, I am so disoriented. And I am so mad every nerve in my body is sparking. If at that moment Chase appeared, I would go for his throat without giving him time to defend himself.

I am also scared to death. How will I ever explain this to Mom and Dad?

I grip the steering wheel and breathe deeply. Okay, maybe he's just taken off for the night and he'll be back. Maybe he'll be back before my parents are up in the morning. He knows it's breaking bail, that everything in his life—our lives—depends on him sticking around. I start the car. Who am I kidding? He's a crankhead with fifteen hundred dollars in his pocket. He's gone, along with my money.

I call Jack on my cell, but there is no answer. I don't know what else to do or where to go, so I drive to Jade's. Her mother and sister are in bed, but she is up, watching TV.

Sitting at the kitchen table, speaking in a whisper, I tell her what an idiot I am, how stupid I was to be duped by an addict. I'd watched it happen in my house a thousand times. If I'd only gone with him, everything would have turned out differently.

"It's not your fault," she says after I finally stop repeating myself. "You did what you thought was right." She then adds, "I don't know if it helps, and I'm sorry if I sound like a cynic, but I also don't think it would have turned out any differently. Maybe it wouldn't have happened tonight, but eventually, he would have taken off. Obviously, that's what he wanted."

"But I made it so easy for him."

"You can't think like that. You're not dealing with a rational person, so stop beating yourself up."

"Oh, god, what have I done?"

"Gordie." Jade lays her hand across mine. "You are going to have to tell your Mom and Dad."

EIGHT

t's after midnight when I leave Jade's apartment, but I can't go home, not without looking for Chase first. Sitting in Mom's car on the street outside Jade's apartment building, I try Jack's number again.

This time he answers. "Hey," he says, "what's up?"

In as few words as I can, I explain what's happened. I tell him that I took Chase to pay his dealers, but my plan backfired and he took off instead. I finish by saying, "You've got to help me look for him."

There is a pause at the end of the line. No doubt he hears the panic in my voice, but there is the practical side to my request. "But it's a school night. They won't let me go out this late."

Jack's bedroom is in the basement. "Sneak out," I tell him. "I'll be parked in front of the Watts' house in fifteen minutes." I hang up, not wanting to give him a chance to argue.

Fifteen minutes later, Jack is where I asked him to be, sitting on the utility box in front of a hedge at the edge of his neighbor's front yard. He gets in the front seat. "You know I'll be forced to beat on you if my parents find about this. What's going on?"

As I start down Mountain Highway, heading back toward the Second Narrows Bridge, I fill Jack in on the details. I try to word it carefully, or at least so I don't come off like a total fool.

Once I've finished, he neatly sums up what I've said. "Okay, let me get this straight—you gave him two thousand dollars in cash—your cash—and you let him go in the house alone? You idiot! How could you be such a chump? Your parents are going to kill you."

There isn't much I can say. I know it well enough myself.

It's beginning to drizzle. I set the windshield wipers on intermittent. The headlights of oncoming cars dart off the shimmery surface as we cross the bridge. It's dark and gloomy outside, but the mood inside the car is even gloomier as Jack and I discuss how to track down Chase.

"Where are we going?" asks Jack.

There is no point in going back to Burnaby. Chase won't return to that drug house for some time, not now that I know where it is. "Downtown."

"At this time of night? You're crazy. I'll tell you right now these doors are staying locked. And I'm not getting out of this car either. Which means I'm not coming to look for you if—I mean *when* you get rolled."

"You don't have to get out. I just want to drive around. Maybe we'll spot him."

"Just walking down the street?"

"Look, have you got any better ideas? I don't know what else to do."

The rain is no deterrent to the number of bums, junkies and hustlers hanging around the rundown hotels and barred pawnshops along East Hastings. Women and girls, some probably not even as old as us, stroll next to the curb. Life on the street has been brutal, leaving them with missing teeth and skin covered in sores. When we stop at the intersection along Hastings near Main, one of them knocks on the window.

Jack squirms in his seat. "This is really creeping me out. Let's face it, you're not going to find him like this. Come on, Gordie, let's get out of here."

"Ignore her. Just keep your eyes open for Chase." The light turns and I continue driving while scanning the people on either side of the street.

"What are you going to do if you see him? He'll recognize the car. He'll take off before you have a chance to pull over."

I know this. I also know how useless it is to search for him this way. I just don't know what else to do. "I don't know. I just know I can't go home without him. It will kill them and they'll hate me."

"Hate you? You were trying to help. If you don't mind my saying, this whole thing doesn't make any sense."

"Nothing makes sense in my house anymore, but that's what will happen."

We are stopped at another traffic light. In the doorway of a boarded-up building an addict is shooting up. He fumbles with his sleeve, but he can't get it up fast enough. Finally he hits his mark and the drug rushes through him. As he leans back against the building, the needle slips from his hand to the sidewalk. "God, what a life," mumbles Jack.

The light turns and we have just started moving again when I am sure I see him, standing on the corner with two other guys. "There he is!" I hit the brakes and swerve sharply to the curb.

Jack looks back to where I'm pointing, to the three guys standing together, hands stuffed in their pockets, hair dripping, no jackets. Their shirts are soaked through and clinging to their chests. "Where? I don't see him."

"He's behind the guy with his back facing us. He's in the shadows—the skinny guy with the dark T-shirt."

"It's not him."

At that moment, the guy with his back to us turns to shout at someone on the other side of the street.

"See?" says Jack.

He's right. The one in the shadows isn't Chase.

But the guy who is shouting comes closer to our car. He seems to be saying something to us. I get Jack to roll down the window to hear what he's saying, maybe he knows something that could help us find Chase. But before either of us has a chance to react, his head is suddenly inside the car; his oversized pupils peer wildly out of a waxy ghoulish face.

It takes Jack a few seconds to find the words, but when he does he sounds as disgusted as he does terrified. "Get out of here!"

The guy begins fumbling with the handle as he tries to open the door. When it doesn't give, he weaves a gnarled hand through the window and attempts to pull the lock.

Jack gets hold of his wrist and wrestles with him. He manages to get his hand away from the lock. "Go, Gordie! Drive!"

I can't just pull back into the traffic—not without the guy's head coming along with us. "Get out, you nutcase!" I yell.

Realizing our predicament and that we can't go anywhere with the man's head still inside, Jack shoves his hand in his face. He pushes him hard, and he stumbles backward to the curb. I step on the gas and speed back into traffic.

"Are you satisfied?" Jack barks. He sinks back against the seat like he's just missed being hit by a train.

"Can we go home, now? I've got to sterilize my hand." Jack holds his hand in the air like he's been crippled.

I don't answer.

"Come on, Gordie, this is not only dangerous, it's a waste of time. You'd be better off to go home and make some phone calls. Call Ryan Linscott."

I know Jack is right. It's a suicide mission to go home, but to take off, or to just not tell my parents what happened would be the kind of thing that Chase would pull. We drive back to the North Shore in silence. I drop Jack off in front of the Watts' house. Pulling his jacket over his head, he sprints toward his house. I watch him disappear around the back where he is headed for the basement door.

I continue driving down the street, turn the corner and pull into the deserted parking lot of an elementary school. It's after midnight, but I still decide to follow Jack's suggestion and call Ryan's house. I dial directory assistance to get the number and then have them connect me. The phone rings many times before it is answered.

"What is it?"

It's Mrs. Linscott's voice—tired and annoyed.

"Is Ryan there?"

"No, he's not. And I don't want you calling here again. Ryan wants nothing to do with you."

For an instant, I am taken aback at how sharp and distant she is. But of course, it doesn't take me long to realize why. She'd recognized the last name on the call display. "I'm sorry for bothering you so late, Mrs. Linscott. This is not Chase Jessup. This is his brother, Gordie. I'm trying to find him. I just thought Ryan might know where he is."

There is a long pause, before a slightly kinder Mrs. Linscott says, "I'm sorry, I thought you were your brother. No, we haven't heard from him. Ryan is in a rehabilitation clinic, and to be honest, we really don't want him to have anything to do with Chase again."

I am surprised and, in a weird way, somewhat envious to hear that Ryan has actually followed through on what he said he was going to do. I thank Mrs. Linscott. I then tell her that I completely understand; my parents would say the same thing.

I start driving again, but I just can't bring myself to go home. Every time I imagine facing my parents and telling them what happened, my heart speeds up and my stomach twists into a knot. Twenty minutes later I am cruising past the park where Harris was found bleeding to death. If Harris hung out there, Chase might also have done so in the past. But I really didn't think he would return so close to home tonight.

It is no longer raining, but the night is overcast and the air is still heavy with moisture. In the distance, on the other side of Burrard Inlet, the lights of the city are muted by fog. The park is illuminated by only a few small halos of yellow cast by the streetlights.

I see figures moving near the bushes. Are they imagined or are they ghosts? Harris come back; even death couldn't end his habit? A light flares—a match leaping to life—and the pinprick end of a cigarette glows. Someone is sitting on the bench. I consider going over to be certain it isn't Chase, but I can already see that it isn't by the shape of the head.

On the way home, I pull into the parking lot of the shopping mall near our house. It's an ordinary collection of buildings, a gray L-shaped block made up of a grocery store, a convenience store, a drug store, a small restaurant, a dry cleaner, a hair salon and a department store at one end.

Sitting in the empty parking lot, I recall a conversation I had many months earlier with Chase. He'd just come back from one of his stints in rehab, and Mom was reluctant to let him out of her sight. Chase nagged until she'd finally agreed to let him pick up a few things at the grocery store. "All right, but don't be any longer than an hour. Here's my list."

Chase was gone for even less. He'd still come home high. I couldn't believe that he'd been able to find drugs so fast and my surprise must have shown on my face.

"I can score anywhere at anytime, Gordie boy," he told me. He'd then followed me into my bedroom where he continued to babble in his arrogant spaced-out way. "You have no idea how easy it is. I had to go no further than our friendly neighborhood mall."

I told him to get lost.

"You know, you are such a baby sometimes. You should hang around with your big brother once in a while. You'd learn a lot. You'd get some street smarts."

He'd said it like it was something I really lacked. It struck me how disconnected we'd become, how we lived in the same house but in two very different worlds. "What for?" I'd asked. "I don't hang around the streets."

I think now that if Harris had had what Chase called street smarts, it sure didn't do him any good.

The neon light above the convenience store blinks. I can no longer avoid going home and telling my parents. They will probably be asleep, which will give me until the morning to think of what to say. Five minutes later I pull into our garage. I close the kitchen door, turn out the light in the front entrance, walk past the living room and down the dark hall toward the stairs and my room.

"That was a long movie."

Dad's voice frightens me almost more than anything has tonight. I return to the living room where I can see him sitting in his favorite armchair in the dark. He switches on the table lamp next to where he sits. "Where's Chase?"

I figure I might as well get right to the point. "He took off. I've been all over the city looking for him."

For the first fifteen years of my life, I'd thought that only mothers cried. I'd learned differently over the past two years. But I'd never seen Dad's eyes fill with tears as quickly as they did at that moment. I was braced for a lot of yelling and questions: Why had I let him take off? Why wasn't I watching him? Instead, Dad speaks as steadily and as evenly as his emotions will allow. "No luck?"

I shake my head, no.

Mom appears in the doorway between the dining room and living room. She strikes me as old, older than I've ever noticed before. I'm not sure if it's the light, but her hair is no longer blond but gray. She holds her dressing gown tightly to her body as if it might help keep away the world's troubles, or at the very least, ours. It's apparent she's been crying, her face is pink and swollen, and she's clutching a ball of tissue in one hand. When she sees Chase isn't with me, she starts softly crying again. I look from Mom to Dad. I wonder how they could just know he would take off, and if they knew, why did they let us go? They were obviously waiting up and they were already extremely upset.

"We had a visit from the police tonight," Dad explains, "a little more than an hour ago."

I catch my breath. So this is it. Something like what had happened to Harris has finally happened to Chase. That's the reason for the state they are in.

But even that might have been better news than what the police had really come to say.

"The man that Chase assaulted, Richard Cross, has died."

Mom's sobs are suddenly punctuated by a loud moan as she turns and leaves the room.

I am stunned. So many emotions roar through me that I can't get a grip on just one. "What does this mean?"

"It means that the charges against Chase have been upgraded to second degree murder. We were to return him to the custody of the police as soon as he came home tonight. He'll have to apply for bail again, but aside from that, it's very likely he will be facing serious prison time. He did kill a man."

It's suddenly all so strange, like I'm watching what's happening from a theater seat. My brother isn't really a meth head—he never has been. He's never lied or stolen anything, and I haven't really just been told that he's murdered a man. And my dad—he isn't really sitting there, flushed from crying, looking like his life has come to an end. I've created the whole crazy skit. But why would I do that?

My mind goes white, like a sheet of lightning. An image flashes across it—Richard Cross's wife and little girl in the lobby of the hospital. The drawings of the unicorns taped above his bed. The man with the bandage around his head is no longer alive. The machines that had been hooked up to him no longer pump and hum.

I drop into the chair across from Dad and cover my face with my hands. Moments later, I feel his hand on my shoulder. "You may as well go to bed, Gordie. Nothing's going to change tonight."

"His drug dealers were after him," my voice comes out muffled through my hands. "I thought if I paid them off, it would be done. You and Mom wouldn't have to know about it. We could all go on from there."

He sighs. Kneeling down next to me he squeezes my shoulder. "You too, huh? How much did you lose?"

"Everything I had. Two thousand, including the money Nana sent me for my birthday."

Dad groans. "Well, I wish I could say I'd reimburse you, but I can't. Not now anyway and probably not for some time."

I feel a pain deep in my gut—like a raw wound I can't reach and can do nothing about.

I wish Chase was dead. I wish he'd disappear off the face of the earth instead of this—the way he keeps coming back, over and over. It's like torture; he's dragging us down along with him, slowly, and we can't fight back because we don't think like him and we never know which direction he'll be coming from next.

I guess that's because what we want and hope for are so different. We always hope it will get better, that he'll change, while he only hopes he can find that next fix.

NINE

The following morning, the stunned and terrified silence I'd come home to the night before has passed. Mom is angry. She starts in on me as soon as I walk into the kitchen. By the way she talks you'd think I'd been Chase's accomplice, maybe even encouraged him to take off.

"You knew he was barely holding on. And to take him directly to those horrible men and then give him so much money! What did you think would happen? What was going through your head? Did you want him to get into trouble?"

I want to remind her that he was already in the worst kind of trouble there is and that I'd certainly played no part in that. But she is in no mood to listen to reason, so I simply say, "I was only trying to help."

"Help! Help him get addicted again?"

Okay, that I couldn't leave alone. "Do you really think that if it was stuck under his nose he would have turned it down?"

At that moment Dad walks into the room. "Arguing is not going to help," he snaps.

Mom glares at him before turning back to the sink. It's obvious that neither of them have slept. For that matter, neither have I. I'd drifted off once or twice only to wake up in the middle of a bad dream, soaked in sweat. Fully awake, I remembered the bad dream was all too true.

Dad is not going to work today. He's going to meet with the police and talk to Chase's lawyer. He wants to find out if there is any chance that the charge against Chase can be downgraded to manslaughter. If he's convicted of manslaughter rather than murder, the amount of time he spends in prison could be substantially less.

Mom says that if ever there was a case that should be downgraded, it's Chase's.

"From our point of view, yes, but it might be hard to convince a jury. Richard Cross did die as a result of what Chase did. He didn't take the man's money, but because he's a drug addict, to a jury it will appear that it was done during the commission of a crime."

"But it wasn't murder," Mom insists. "He didn't mean to do it. It was the drugs."

"That's no excuse!" argues Dad.

Mom is silent. Dad pours a cup of coffee. He sits at the table across from where I'm moving cereal around in a bowl.

"Look, a man is dead. You're going to have to get it through your head that Chase is responsible. It doesn't matter to the man's family if Chase planned it, if he was on drugs, or if the devil himself handed him the weapon; the result is still the same to them."

There is less than a month left of school. Jack reminds me of this as we walk down the hall toward our lockers. I groan, because it suddenly occurs to me how I've let my schoolwork slide. I've completely forgotten that I have an English essay due today and I now discover that I'm two units behind in chemistry.

Jack sighs. "But I was hoping you could explain that last one to me. I thought we'd skip Spanish and go through it. Well, that's it, I guess I'm going down with you." He closes his locker door and threads the lock in place. "So, did Chase ever show up?"

As we walk to Spanish class I tell Jack that he hasn't, that Richard Cross has died and about the new charges.

"He died? Wow, how are you dealing with that?"

"Well, let me see: Mom blames me for Chase taking off, Dad's a wreck and can't think about anything else, and now I'm way behind in school. I guess from any angle," I say, "not very well."

Ms. Fraser agrees to give me an extension on the English essay, but I'm dead in chemistry. Mr. Saik gives us a pop quiz on the last two units, and I'm pretty much clueless. Jack looks over at me. He taps his pencil against his desk, frowning like he's also screwed, and it's all my fault.

I spend the next few days holed up in the basement trying to concentrate on my homework, but it's impossible to ignore the arguing coming from upstairs. The silence is just about as unbearable. When it becomes too much to ignore, I pick up my bass and crank up my amp until the whole house reverberates just so I don't go out of my mind.

Over the next week, Chase doesn't call or show up. The police check every day to see if he's contacted us. They tell Dad they continue to check all the known drug houses, but so far he hasn't turned up.

Mom spends her days driving around the city in search of him. She doesn't tell us where she goes, but we have a good idea. Dad tells her that what she's doing is dangerous. Other than that, he doesn't try to stop her, and anyway, she ignores what he says.

She carries a photo of Chase, not a recent photo, but an older picture in which his face looks healthy and he has a full set of teeth. There is no point in telling her that no one will recognize him from that.

My history final is scheduled for the morning of June 12. After walking into the kitchen to grab a bite to eat before school, I come across Mom sitting blurry-eyed and sobbing at the table. I've reached the point where I don't say anything—there is no point asking why today is any worse than yesterday. I pour myself a glass of juice.

"Do you know what today is?" she asks.

I shrug. "It's the twelfth."

She is holding something, a folded piece of paper. I glance at the envelope on the table in front of her. It's an old letter from Chase. The postmark tells me it was written when he was at boy scout camp.

"It's Chase's eighteenth birthday."

"Oh, right," I say. I had forgotten.

"I always thought he'd be in university by now, or at least heading off. He'd have his whole life ahead of him, a career—your dad and I always thought he'd be good at business. He was so bright and personable even as a little boy. Maybe he'd get married." She starts to cry.

"Mom," I say, but I stop at that. There really is nothing more to be said.

She wipes her cheek with the palm of her hand. "The prosecuting lawyer and the family are applying to have Chase's case moved to adult court."

"What does that mean?"

"It means that if they're successful, he'll be tried as if he were an adult, even though the incident happened when he was technically still a youth."

She still refers to Chase cracking Richard Cross over the head with a bottle as "the incident." Even now that the man has died.

"If he's convicted," she continues, "he'll go to prison with men who have committed the most horrible crimes."

She is obviously waiting for some reassurance, or at least a reaction. But what can I say? Chase too has committed the most horrible of crimes. "That would suck," is all I can think of to say.

She looks over at me. "It would suck? That's all you can say, Gordie? Your brother is likely to go to prison where he could be beaten and abused, and that's all you have to say?"

"What do you want me to say? I can't change the law. If that's the way it works, how can I change anything?"

"You could care!"

"I do care."

"Well, you sure don't show it. You don't talk about it. You don't discuss how we're going to find him or how we're going to get him home. In fact, if it wasn't for you—if you hadn't taken Chase out that night, he'd still be here."

"Yeah," I said, "and Richard Cross would still be dead!"

Mom glares at me before she starts to cry again. I hadn't meant to hurt her, but how can she possibly blame me? And why is it that Chase is the good guy and I'm the rotten one? I heft my backpack over my shoulder and leave.

I totally screw up my exam. I can't concentrate; dates and battles all run together, and I can't write a sentence that makes any sense. For the first time in my life I worry about whether or not I'm going to pass a course rather than just how well I've done.

Two days later we get the news that the prosecutor has been successful. If Chase hadn't taken off he might have had a chance, but the judge rules he will be tried in adult court. Mom and Dad are devastated; not only will his sentence likely be much stiffer and he'll have to serve it in prison, but he can now be named in news reports.

Dad sits with his head in his hands after reading the story the following morning. It is the first time Chase's name has appeared in print. It's a Saturday. Within an hour the phone rings several times: Grandma, Aunt Gail, friends and neighbors, people Dad works with; a few even come by the house. They are all so solemn, like we've lost a member of the family, which I suppose, in a way, we have.

Monday morning I am sitting in physics, the only class I'm not flunking, when something brushes against my shoulder. I look down. A paper airplane has landed on my desk. Mr. Dublenko has his back to the class as he works through a problem on the whiteboard. I turn around to see Jason Dodds and Brian Zimmerman where they sit at the back of the class, smirking. Dodds tips back on two legs of his chair. "Psycho," he hisses.

I unfold the airplane. It is the newspaper story about Chase.

"Mr. Jessup."

I look up. Mr. Dublenko is standing next to my desk.

"Perhaps you'd like to share your airmail with the rest of the class."

I swear, teachers are born with an extra hinge in the back of the necks. How else could he have possibly seen that and been next to my desk so fast?

"No," I say, "I'd rather not." I smash the paper into a wad and stuff it in my binder. Before he has a chance to send me out of the room, I pick up my books and leave the class.

I don't really blame Mr. Dublenko. I like him, but he's one of those guys who is so absorbed in his subject that he probably reads nothing but textbooks from morning until night. I'm sure he knows nothing about Chase. What really surprises me is that Dodds or Zimmerman actually read the newspaper.

Half an hour later Ms. Larson tracks me down in the library. "I had a call from Mr. Dublenko," she says. "Will you come down to my office? I'd like to talk." Ms. Larson looks like a new blossom in old snow. Her dress is crimson, a bright spot against the backdrop of old books, and she wears a silky white handkerchief around her neck.

"It was really no big deal," I tell her. "I'll be there tomorrow. I just don't want to go back to class right now."

She shakes her head. "It's more than that, Gordie. We need to talk. I'm afraid you didn't do very well on your last two exams."

"Yeah, I know. All right." I get up and walk with her to her office.

"Have a seat," she says. She sits at her desk but pulls her chair out from behind it so she is sitting across from me.

"I'm concerned," she begins, "because it's not like you to do so poorly. Now, I'm not trying to pry, but I understand your brother has got himself into some trouble. Do you think that might be affecting your work?"

Affecting? How about the cause of it!

"Yes," I say, "it's a little difficult to concentrate, to say the least."

She leans forward, laying her hand across my arm. "Would you feel comfortable talking about it?"

Her silver bracelet is cool against my skin. Again, I think how telling her about Chase would be like spitting in her face. Everything he's done and turned into is so ugly. She is so tidy and neat. I shrug. "There's not a lot to say. I would like to know if I have any options."

Ms. Larson straightens, but her tone doesn't change. She doesn't seem angry that I don't want to talk about it. "Of course. I've talked to your teachers. Mr. Saik is willing to give you a make-up exam and Ms. Fraser will postpone the *Hamlet* essay. My only concern is whether your circumstances will change enough to allow you to study the material. If you don't think it's likely, or that you could be ready in a week, you might have to take summer school."

Summer school? Only losers have to repeat a course in summer school. "I'll take a shot at the exams."

Ms. Larson says she will set them up. She then tells me to try and concentrate on my own health. Not that I should ignore the problems around me, but there are circumstances where we need to look out for ourselves first.

It is nearly eight o'clock when I head home from work two days later. The first thing I notice when I approach the house is that the side door to the garage is ajar. I stick my head inside. The garage is empty, which means my parents aren't at home. The door between the garage and house is open—the lock has been jimmied. The pocketknife Dad keeps on his workbench lies on the garage floor. This is my first clue. Chase knows the lock is faulty and that the knife works if it is used in a certain way.

I push the door open slowly. He might still be in the house, and there is no telling what state he will be in. He's desperate; there's no question about that. Why else would he risk showing up at home with the entire city police force looking for him? The kitchen is the first room I enter, and it's a shambles, like it has been ransacked by a hungry bear. The refrigerator and the cupboard doors are all open: wrappers and scraps and peels, shrunken from hours exposed to the air, are scattered across the floor. Chase has pigged-out, probably just after Mom had left, earlier in the morning. He was coming down from a long high, tweaking, ready to crash, which would explain his desperation and his appetite.

I pass through the rest of the house in a daze. I can't even guess what is missing from Mom and Dad's room, but it has been torn apart. Mom's jewelry box has been dumped upside down on her dresser. The doors of Dad's armoire are open and the contents are strewn across the floor. I continue down the hall to the living room.

The destruction is erratic, and it would have required a huge amount of strength to shatter and overturn some of the things he did. I walk gingerly around the broken fragments of the glass coffee table to where the stereo cabinet lays on its side. Adjacent to the fireplace, a very large bookshelf that had been bolted to the wall has been ripped off, and I wonder what he expected to find. I step over the heap of books and smashed ornaments on my way to the dining room.

Suddenly I turn and tear down the stairs to my own bedroom, my heart beating hard in my chest. My blood freezes and my stomach flips. A hole has been punched through my closet door, and what is left of it hangs from one hinge. My Fender Precision bass is gone. I feel like I've been punched in the stomach and my insides pulled out. I smash the door so that it falls right off, and I sink onto my bed.

Dad arrives home fifteen minutes later. To my surprise, he immediately calls the police. When two cops show up less than ten minutes later, Dad is heartsick but matter-of-fact. He tells them he suspects it was his son. He then writes down what he believes is missing.

I wonder how long my guitar will keep Chase high. How wrecked can he get on the money he gets for it and for how long—maybe a day. Certainly not anywhere near as long as it took me to earn the money to buy it.

Mom does not return home until nearly midnight. Her face is bloodless and her voice trembles; no doubt a combination of stress and the things she's seen.

I think how she is beginning to resemble the broken-down people she's spending her time with.

"Thank God," she whispers, when Dad tells her about the break-in. "He's still alive."

TEN

Two days after the break-in, Ryan Linscott calls me from rehab. "I read about Chase in the paper," he tells me. "If you're still looking for him, I can give you the names of some places he might be hanging out."

"All right," I say, although I am sure that most of them are already known to the police. But aside from the drug houses, he mentions a number of public places and a couple of abandoned lots. I write them all down and ask him how he is making out.

"It's rough," he says. "All day I try to think of other things, but at night I still dream about getting high. And then I want it so bad. Or I get a whiff of something that reminds me of the smell and I crave it like nothing else. I've got three weeks left. I'm hoping these feelings are gone by the time I leave this place."

I tell him that I hope they are too. I don't tell him that they never went away with Chase.

"What keeps me going right now is thinking about how it destroyed Harris and Chase."

"Yeah, and everybody they came in contact with."

We say good-bye. I have just hung up when the phone rings again. It stops after one ring. Mom must have grabbed it upstairs just as I reached it. I don't recognize the number on the call display. Ten minutes later, it rings again. This time it's Jack who's phoning to let me know we have a practice.

"And what am I going to play?"

"Oh, man," he moans, "I forgot that lunatic walked off with your P-bass." He's silent a moment before it hits him. "How are you going to play in the battle of the bands?"

I've been struggling with this for two days. I have no money to buy even a crummy secondhand bass, forget anything classic like what I'd had. And although I've begged Dad, he refuses to tell his insurance company about the break-in. If they find out it was his own son who ransacked the house—a drug addict wanted for murder—he's afraid they'll drop all his policies, never mind simply raising his rates.

"I guess I'm not."

"Come on, Gordie. You can't let this stop you."

"What do you suggest I do? I have no money."

"What do you mean you have no money? You've got a job."

"Do I have to remind you what happened to my money so you can tell me again how stupid I was?"

Jack moans again. "We can't do it without you. Okay, look, we'll figure something out."

I've just hung up when Mom suddenly announces that she has to go out.

"But I have to work in an hour. Dad doesn't want the house left empty."

"I'll be home in twenty minutes." She seems almost nervous as she grapples for her keys, so I don't say anything more when she grabs her purse and leaves the house.

She *is* home in less than twenty minutes. She isn't carrying any bags or packages when she comes through the door, which makes me wonder where she'd gone. But I'm already pressed for time, so I don't ask. I leave for work.

The routine of stocking shelves and checking out hardware is a relief from the chaos of home. The loss of my guitar continues to be a raw spot in my stomach, but it isn't until six hours later when I'm walking home from the bus stop and spot the For Sale sign on our front lawn that it takes its next direct punch.

At least Dad had warned me before he'd sold his sports car, but he'd said nothing about selling the house.

"I have no choice," he tells me once I'm in the house.

"But the house, Dad? Where are we going to live?"

"I haven't thought that far ahead." Dad runs his hand through his hair, which is uncharacteristically long.

"But with Chase skipping bail," he continues, "and the cost of lawyers fees, we've already cashed in every-thing else."

My loathing for Chase and all he's done seethes so close to the surface I think I might have a seizure. Where is that bloodsucking jerk? No doubt he's lying in some flea-infested meth house, spaced-out, tracing his fingers on the floor. My mother doesn't need to worry about the criminals in prison getting hold of him. Not if I get to him first.

I skip school on Monday. I spend the day going to pawn-shops and secondhand stores trying to track down my guitar. I start downtown, at the East End pawnshop where Dad and I had found his watches. There are dozens of guitars, some well-worn, some nearly new, but no sign of my P-bass. There are also hundreds of gold chains, bracelets and wedding rings, abandoned for a few hits.

I approach the clerk sitting behind the display case. Perhaps he can tell me if he's recently bought and sold a bass. "It's sunburst," I say. "Only six months old, in perfect shape. It would have been brought in by a skinny guy with gray eyes and brown hair. Oh, and sores all over his face."

The clerk is polishing a silver bracelet. An old man, he glances up at me with faded eyes. "Do you know how many guys like that I see in a day? I don't remember your guitar."

I take one last look around and head to the next shop. From one dismal barred window to the next, I search for my P-bass. I ignore the panhandlers, the rubbies with their hands out. At one time I would have laid a dollar in their hands, but my attitude has changed toward all of them.

"Hey, sweetheart."

It's a man's voice, close enough that I turn. Surely it couldn't have been meant for me. A guy with the jaundiced complexion and shrunken form of a junkie, maybe thirty, speaks again. "Want a date?"

He has no teeth, and the odor coming from him makes my stomach churn. I glance behind me, but with no one close by, it appears that he really is talking to me. I ask him if he is.

"Twenty bucks," he says.

I glare at him. The idea is more revolting than anything I've ever heard. My first thought is to swing at him, to pound him out, but even one blow would probably kill him. He interprets my hesitation as a chance to barter.

"Okay, I'll make it fifteen. It'll be worth every cent, guaranteed." His nose drips, and with no teeth, his grin is creepily cartoonish. I am living a nightmare. He takes a step closer.

The smell overwhelms me. "One more step and I'll grind you into this sidewalk."

Instantly his hands shoot up. "Okay, okay," he says, taking a few steps back. Standing with his back against a boarded-up building, his eyes dart in the opposite direction down the street. He is not surprised by my reaction, and if he had expected it, it hadn't stopped him from trying. Maybe that's how he'd lost at least some of his teeth.

I am thoroughly creeped out. Is that how Chase makes his money when he can't find anything to steal? The thought is so repulsive I have to stop and steady myself to keep from throwing up. I don't stop long at any of the remaining pawnshops, just long enough to see that my bass isn't around.

On the off chance that Chase hasn't taken my guitar downtown, I decide to look in the secondhand stores on the North Shore. I spot my bass in the window of the first store I check out. As a new acquisition, it must have rated a bit of marketing. I stare at it. It's mine, there is no doubt; I recognize the wearing of the frets. A bell jingles as I open the door to the store. I ask the clerk the price.

"Fifteen hundred," he grunts. His long gray hair is twisted into a braid that extends halfway down his back, but his face is clean shaven. He's working on a cross-word puzzle. I don't know why it strikes me as an odd thing for a guy who runs a secondhand shop to do.

I don't argue, but I do ask if he remembers the guy who sold it to him.

He doesn't take much time to remember. "Not a clue."

"You must have the ticket," I persist.

Turning toward the bass propped in the window, he changes his mind. "On second thought, I do remember. It was a woman. A woman brought that in, a tall redhead. She said it was her boyfriend's and they were through. She'd kicked him out and kept it for the rent he owed her. She's not going to want it back. You want to try it out? Fourteen hundred for you."

I shake my head. "Not right now. But would you hold it for me? I should have the money in a month."

Frowning, he takes in the contents of the room with one sweep of his tattooed arm. "Look around you. Does this look like Wal-Mart? I don't put anything on hold. I also don't do exchanges or refunds if things don't fit. You buy it, it's yours. You don't buy it, it goes to the first person that does. Does that make sense?"

I nod. I can't look at my bass when I step onto the street, although I want to smash that window and take back what's rightfully mine.

I kick the For Sale sign on my way across our front yard. It doesn't budge, but it does leave me with a throbbing toe.

Jade has called while I was out. I call her back. Just hearing her voice lifts some of the layers of my dark mood. She offers to help me study that night, so I ask Mom if I can borrow her car. She agrees. I am just about to leave when the phone rings again. Thinking it might be Jade with a change of plans, I race back and pick it up.

It is a familiar voice. I suck in my breath. "Mom, I need forty bucks. Can you meet me?"

My brother. I want to blast him. But I don't say anything, because Mom has picked up another phone and she begins to speak. Her voice is a nervous whisper.

"When, Chase?"

"In five minutes. At the shopping mall."

"But I can't get there that fast. I've just given Gordie the car. I'll have to walk. It will take me at least twenty minutes."

"Get him to drop you off. You can walk back. Please, I'm starving. I need something to eat. I haven't eaten all day."

"I can bring you some sandwiches. I can bring some cheese and fruit and some canned food to tide you over for a few days."

Chase is quick to say, "No." But it takes him a little longer to think up some lame reason why this wouldn't be a good idea. "It's better if you just give me the money. I have no place to store food."

"Chase, I told you not to call me after five. What if your Dad answers?"

"I know, but I'm hungry."

"You said you'd come with me to the police station. Will you come this time?"

"No, I told you I'll go when I'm ready."

"When?"

"I don't know. When I'm ready."

Mom sighs. "You're only making it harder for yourself. If you turn yourself in, it would be in your favor."

"I'm working toward it. I don't feel very good. It will be soon, I promise. When I feel better. So, will you bring me the money?"

"You're not going to feel better living like this." There is a pause before Mom continues. "Will you at least tell me where you're staying?" Her voice sounds so frail that I am all at once sorry for her, despite how pathetic the call is, and how she just can't say no to Chase. "I only want to know so I can know you're safe."

"I'm not staying in one place. I'll see you in five minutes. I'll be in the usual place."

Chase hangs up. I check previous calls. The same phone number—five, six times the day before, four times the day before that. Mom has been meeting Chase and giving him money.

I don't know what I will say, but I have to find out what Mom is going to do. Dad is not home yet, or she would take his car to meet Chase. I walk upstairs. I find her in the kitchen just hanging up the phone.

"I'm leaving. Is there anything you need before I go?" I glance at the phone book on the table in front of her—the yellow pages are open to the list of taxicabs. "Do you need to go somewhere?" I jangle the keys in my pocket. I am nervous and angry. I need to know if she will tell me the truth.

She shakes her head and then turns her back to me, waving me away with her free hand. There are tears in her eyes, and I know then I can't confront her. The whole thing of Chase calling and the secret she's forced to keep is killing her too.

The drive to Jade's apartment gives me time to think about everything that's going on. I think I might go crazy. Not only is my brother a murderer, but I have just learned that my mother is an accessory to his crime. Even if she doesn't know where he is most of the time, she does know where he can be found in those few minutes that she meets him at the mall. The detective who drops by every day has warned us about doing exactly what she's doing—withholding information that would make us liable.

I then begin wondering where she's getting the money. Forty dollars, three or four times a day for the past week adds up to a fair bit. My parents are already so broke they are selling the house, so where is she getting the cash?

I arrive at Jade's. Sitting at the kitchen table, she quizzes me from the chapter summaries in my history textbook. With all the stuff that's already whirring around inside my head, and now, searching for answers, I feel like my brain is in a blender. I do abysmally.

"Gordie," she says, "I thought you were going to go through this stuff. Your exam is tomorrow. And have you read *Hamlet* yet?"

"I haven't had a chance." Which isn't quite true. It's just been really hard to get into the Prince of Denmark and all his family troubles when mine are in the twenty-first century and staring me in the face.

She drops the book to her lap. "Okay, what's wrong? Something's really bugging you."

I can't tell her. This latest thing involving my mother—I can't tell anyone until I can get my own mind around it. I guess it's partially a matter of pride, although I'm surprised that I have any left. Whatever, I just can't bring myself to tell Jade. "You know what's wrong," I say. "I live in a nuthouse."

Her eyes narrow. "No, there's something more than that."

"No, there isn't. Okay, yes, there is. I'll tell you what's driving me crazy. I found my bass today."

Jade smiles a little. "But that's a good thing, isn't it? Or is something wrong with it? Is it damaged?"

"No, it looks good. It's perfect. As far as I can tell there's not a scratch. It's just that it's in a pawnshop where it's selling for fifteen hundred dollars."

Jade groans.

"Never mind. I'll just have to live with it like everything else. Now shoot—what's the next question?"

It's nearly midnight when I get home. Mom and Dad are in bed. I sit at the kitchen table, a glass of water in front of me, staring at the business card on the fridge in the light of the range hood. *Detective Jim Keppler*, it says. *Homicide*. He'd left it in case we heard from Chase. We were to let him know immediately—anytime, anything that would help bring in Chase.

Tomorrow—tomorrow I will speak to Dad. I pour the glass of water into the sink. Once in my bedroom, I throw the textbooks and review sheets off my bed, flop across it and turn out the light.

Crap. I have two exams the following day, and I'm not ready for either one. Summer school is a given.

ELEVEN

There is no point putting myself through the humiliation of blowing both exams and then being called to the office to learn the pathetic results. The next morning I go straight to Ms. Larson's office.

"Gordie," she says brightly. "Come in and sit down. Are you ready to write your exams today?"

I hate to say no and watch her warm smile splutter to a deflated frown. But I'm going to have to disappoint her at some point. I do as she asks and sit across from her. "No, I'm not. That's what I've come to talk to you about. I just haven't had time to study. I've come to sign up for summer school."

Ms. Larson looks disappointed but not all that surprised. "Hmm," she says, "that's not very good news."

She is right about that, particularly for me. I look at my feet. The inner seam of my left shoe has split and is coming away from the sole. I cover it with my right foot.

Ms. Larson rises from her desk and quietly closes the door. She returns to her chair. "I've been meaning to ask you something. How are things at school? Are you being treated okay? I mean, since the news of your brother's circumstances was published, are the other students treating you all right?"

"I haven't had any problems." Which, with the exception of Zimmerman and Dodds, is true.

Ms. Larson nods. "That's good. Well, I could talk to your teachers and we could set another date. There is still a week left of school."

I'm already shaking my head. "It's not going to happen. I know I won't get to it. There's too much going on right now."

"Like what?" Ms. Larson's voice is soft.

I finally look up. I had not come to her office to tell her, but somehow it's different this time. When I look across the desk, I don't notice how her clothes match or how precisely she shuffles the papers. I see someone just waiting for me to tell her about Chase's phone calls and the danger Mom's putting herself in. So I spill it. I tell her all that and then about how I know I have to tell Dad but I don't know how, and that my life is falling apart.

When I'm finished and I'm staring at my broken shoe again, Ms. Larson is quiet for a time. She then says, "Gordie, look at me."

I try.

"You are right. You do have to tell your father. Your Mom has been put in a position she can't cope with and she needs your help."

She goes on to say many other things too, about how well I'm handling the situation and that I shouldn't feel guilty or responsible for anything because what has happened is beyond my control. She finishes by asking, "Will you let me know how it goes once you've talked to your dad?"

I nod. Ms. Larson says good luck, stands up and shakes my hand. "And if you're certain you won't have time to study, I'll register you for summer school."

I'm not sure why I feel forty pounds lighter when I leave her office. It has just been confirmed that I've flunked two courses, and I'll be spending July in a hot sweaty classroom, dodging Zimmerman and Dodds' spitballs, but I feel good. Until I get home from school and spot the police car parked outside our house.

When I walk in the door, I discover two cops—one of them is Detective Keppler—sitting at the kitchen table across from Mom and Dad. As it turns out, I didn't have to break the news to Dad; the police have somehow found out that Chase was contacting Mom. She looks miserable. She is trying to explain why she'd done it, but the police do not appear all that sympathetic. I grab a banana from the bowl on the counter. Fresh fruit—something rare in our house. Dad must have gone shopping. I am heading for my room when Detective Keppler calls me back.

"Gordie, you may as well stay. You all have to know how serious this is."

Reluctantly I return to the kitchen, where I stand with my back against the counter. I peel the banana and take a bite.

"He kept saying he'd come with me to the police station," Mom sobs, barely audible above the sound of the old coffeemaker. "I thought that I could eventually talk him into it. If I'd cut him off, I would have lost him completely."

The younger cop shuffles his feet beneath the chair.

Detective Keppler ignores her excuses. "What time does he usually call in the morning?"

Mom rubs her forehead and sighs. "He's been calling not long after Gordie leaves for school. Around nine o'clock, I guess."

"Okay, we know he has been calling from the phone booth outside the drug store at the mall. Tomorrow when he calls I want you to keep him on the line. We're going to be there."

Mom begins to cry harder. Dad doesn't move to comfort her but says, "She will. I'll stay home to make sure it happens the way you want."

Detective Keppler looks from Mom to Dad. "I'm sorry. But it's the only way. You must realize that we have to bring him in. We don't want anyone else to get hurt, including him. Now, Mrs. Jessup, we are counting on you not to say anything that will alert Chase that we are there."

Dad stands up. "I assure you that she won't."

Once the police are gone, Dad chastises Mom again. "How could you not have told them? You knew you could have gone to jail for that!"

I duck into the basement, wanting to avoid another heated argument. Although I'm not sure why they still bother me. It seems to be the only way we communicate with each other anymore.

The phone rings just as I reach the bottom of the stairs. Closing the door to muffle the argument going on upstairs, I pick it up in the rec room.

"Hi, Gordie, dear."

It's my grandmother in Ontario. "Hi, Nana. How are you?"

"I couldn't be better, although I can't say the same for your grandfather. He came in sixth in his golf tournament this morning, so he's in a bit of a slump. You know how competitive he is."

I chuckle. Yes, I do know how competitive he is.

"Anyway, we are so proud of you. We hear you're playing in a band competition. How is that new guitar?"

Mom hasn't told her about the break-in. Oh well, there's no point in getting into it now. "It's perfect,"

I say, picturing it in the window of the secondhand store.

"Good, good. Maybe you can bring it when you come to visit this summer. We'd love to hear you play. Let me know as soon as you can when you're going to come out, we've got all kinds of things planned. I sent your Mom money last week, five hundred dollars for your flight and five hundred for Chase, just so he has some cash until he finds a job. How is he doing, anyway? Your Mom tells me he's been doing some fix-up jobs around the house since he got out on bail. Has there been any word about the man he hit? Is he recovering?"

I sink into a chair. She doesn't know. Mom hasn't told her that Richard Cross died or that Chase has taken off. I have also just discovered where Mom is getting the two hundred dollars a day she's been giving Chase.

"Nana," I say, "I'm sorry, I'm just on my way to work. I've got to get going. I'm looking forward to seeing you. I'm going to let you talk to Mom."

"Oh, I'm sorry to have kept you, dear. Yes, give me to your mother. You have a good evening at work."

Once I've called Mom to the phone, I avoid her until I go to work. She gave money meant for me to Chase. It's bad enough I have a brother that I can't trust, but my mother?

I go through the motions at work. Jade is not scheduled to work, so it's just me and Ralph. While I work the cash register and help customers find what they are looking for, my mind is really focused on trying to decide where I should stand to watch Chase's arrest. Where will I have the best vantage point, but he won't be able to see me? I decide that the bus shelter across the parking lot from the drug store will allow me to see him but still be an inconspicuous place.

The following morning Dad sits at the kitchen table, turning the pages of the newspaper. Mom paces the floor, glancing at the clock every moment or two. After drinking half a cup of coffee, I throw my backpack over my shoulder like I do every other school day. It's earlier than usual when I leave the house. I need time to get to the bus shelter at the shopping center before Chase calls.

Most of the parking lot is still empty, but outside the drug store and convenience store, which open early, shoppers swing in and out. I scan the parking lot and sidewalks for Chase. Ten minutes after I arrive, I realize that a few of the shoppers have returned to the drug store more than once. Undercover police officers. There are more. Not far from where I sit a couple of men watch the shoppers from inside an unmarked police car. I am sure of it.

Three girls, skipping school, hang around outside the drug store, smoking and chatting. Aside from them,

there are no other young people around—only the odd
one running for the bus shelter, late for school.

I think of my parents waiting impatiently by the
phone as time grinds by. I am glad I am not in the kitchen
with them. My mother would be a whimpering wreck.
I wonder again how long a person can withstand unre-
lenting stress? There has to be a point where the nervous
system shorts out and everything fizzles to a halt.

It's almost nine thirty when I finally spot him. He
comes from behind the department store at the end
of the mall. My brother, who has been the focus of an
intense police search, just appears like he's been set
down around the corner and is now walking toward
the phone booth.

In the two weeks since Chase has taken off, he's
regained that anorexic wasted look. He wears the same
clothes—ripped and filthy now—that he'd had on the
night he took off. He flicks his head repeatedly, and
every now and again he rubs his nose with the back of
his hand.

As he crosses the parking lot, he reminds me of a
withered old lion trying to hunt: back slung low, belly
to the ground, head swiveling to sniff the air. If I didn't
know how destructive he was I might even feel a tinge
of pity for him.

Chase is perhaps a hundred feet from the phone
booth when I notice one of the undercover cops trying

to herd the three girls inside the entrance to the drug store. They are angry at having to butt out their cigarettes. The cop cannot get the girls to cooperate, and another police officer joins her. They have to take the girls by the arms and steer them inside. Chase turns at the scuffle, stops a moment, but moves forward again.

The cops in the car are listening to their radios. I see others speaking to shoppers. The shoppers glance around curiously before heading quickly for the nearest entrance. Fifty feet short of the phone booth, Chase stops walking again. This time, his eyes sweep slowly across the parking lot. They fix on Detective Keppler and another police officer. The two men lean against a car on the other side of the phone booth, as if in conversation. Something has clued him in. Maybe he recognizes them as police officers; whatever it is, paranoia strikes. Suddenly, Chase turns and tears off, back in the direction from which he came.

The cops break into action. The unmarked car in front of me squeals away, and the officers on foot take off after Chase. There are far more of them than I had realized. Chase pushes aside a little girl who is walking next to her mother, throwing her to the sidewalk. The girl screams. A police car parked close to the mall entrance also roars off.

I move from behind the shelter, and I can see Chase dart between cars. He disappears behind an armored truck parked outside a bank; then he reappears, bounding like a jackrabbit. I would never have thought he possessed that kind of physical endurance, but adrenaline can do amazing things. Chase turns the corner behind the department store.

The mall is close to opening, and the police are hindered by shoppers and cars pulling into the parking lot. Radio commands crackle and directions are given. There is confusion. I don't think they ever expected Chase would clue in and run.

As soon as I see him disappear behind the store, I start after him myself. I tear across the parking lot. Car tires squeal as I dart between parking stalls.

"Gordie!" It's Detective Keppler. He is pacing in front of the telephone booth shouting into a radio when he sees me. "Keep back!"

I ignore him. If they can't get him, I will. I turn the corner. There is a short field behind the mall, stretching to the back of a gas station and a body shop. Chase must have already crossed the field. I can see the cops on foot checking between and inside the cars parked behind the body shop. Just south of the gas station is a medical building. I cross the field and run down the alley between the medical building and the gas station, emerging on to the street in front of them. Traffic is heavy. Pedestrians stand at the intersection, waiting for the lights to change. I scan up and down the sidewalk.

There is no sign of Chase and no way to know which way he has gone.

I stand there a moment longer before turning around. I walk back through the alley, my heart thumping, my anger a hard lump in my throat. I kick a garbage can, the sound of metal hitting concrete echoes in my ear. I pull myself up on a giant Dumpster behind the medical building, push back the heavy lid and peer inside. Nothing but garbage. I let the lid slam shut.

"Gordie?"

I slump back against the Dumpster at the sound of Detective Keppler's voice.

"I can't take it anymore," I tell him, letting the back-pack slide off my shoulder. "He's ruined my life. He's ruined my parents' lives." I am so close to blubbering. I take in a deep breath, keeping my eyes fixed on the graffiti on the concrete wall.

The detective puts his hand on my shoulder. "Look, we'll get him. It didn't happen this time, but we will. Things will get better once we do."

I turn away. "Well, they sure as hell can't get any worse. He's taken everything. He's ruined everything. I don't know how they can get better. They'll never be the way they were." My voice is hoarse.

Detective Keppler doesn't say anything right away. How many times has he dealt with guys like Chase, watched the families disintegrate before his eyes?

"The important thing is that he doesn't get to you. Only you can prevent that. Don't let him drag you down along with everything else."

I don't answer.

"Do you hear me, Gordie? You've made it this far."

I nod.

With one hand, he squeezes my shoulder. "Keep your head up. Go to school. Go to the movies and hang out with your friends. Kiss your girlfriend—and if you don't have one, get one. Keep on living your life; it's your best defense. Leave this to us. I promise we'll make things change."

I shoulder my backpack again, nod at Detective Keppler and head back to the bus stop to go to school. I arrive just in time for second block.

"Where were you?" Jack shouts down the nearly empty hallway. He stands next to the doorway to math class while I pull books from my locker. I walk down to meet him.

"I slept in." We enter math class together. "I missed the bus."

Throughout the day, I keep replaying what has happened in my mind. Considering his disadvantages, it's astounding that a messed-up, scramble-brained guy like Chase continues to elude everyone. On the other hand, I guess it isn't. We continue to count on him to act like a rational human being when he is

anything but. Standing before my locker at three
fifteen, I try to remember what books I need for homework. I begin to wonder why I have even bothered to
come to school at all. I can't recall a thing that was said
in class all day.

By the time I arrive home Mom and Dad are not
talking to one another. Still, it is as tense as if I'm
listening to them scream at one another over the sound
of a train. Mom has spent the afternoon driving around
looking for Chase, with no luck. Not long after I get
home from school, she takes off again.

"She blames me," Dad tells me. He stands at the
kitchen counter, spreading mustard on a piece of bread.
He slaps it over the rest of his sandwich. "And the police.
She says that if we'd only left her alone she would have
been able to talk Chase into turning himself in."

"No, she wouldn't," I say.

Dad sits at the table and takes a bite of his sandwich. He chews gingerly before crossing the kitchen
and letting it slide from the plate into the garbage can.
He's become so thin. I suspect that sandwich was probably the only thing he's attempted to eat all day.

"You and I know that."

"What's going to happen now?" Taking the plate
from Dad's hand, I open the dishwasher. The stench of
decaying tuna and cheese makes me take a step back.
There aren't many dishes, but the few that are in there

have been sitting on the rack for days. I add soap and turn the dishwasher on.

Dad shakes his head. "I really don't know. But I'll tell you this, the next time the police have him within their grasp they won't be nearly so kind."

TWELVE

Dad moves downstairs into my territory. He begins using Chase's room to store his stuff, but he sleeps in the rec room. It's strange sharing a space with my father. It's like one of us got caught in a game of Red Rover and we're suddenly on the same side. He and Mom have stopped talking, or at least they say nothing more to each other than what needs to be said. She occupies the upstairs, and Dad and me are down.

Mom acts like we're traitors. She'd had it all under control, she tells Aunt Gail. She would have talked Chase into turning himself in if she'd only had a few more days. She can no longer trust either of us, not now that we've joined forces with the police. Despite Aunt Gail trying to tell her that there are no sides, that we all want only what's best for her and Chase, she remains unconvinced.

Aunt Gail spends more and more time at our house, talking to Mom, trying to get her out of bed and doing something while also acting as a referee. She cleans and cooks. Now and again she makes a comment that leads me to believe that she has no idea how things got to the point they have. She reminds me of myself when Chase first got into drugs, when he first started lying and stealing, and my disbelief that anyone could be so careless toward the people who were trying to help him. Aunt Gail has a lot to learn about crankheads like Chase.

The police drop by to talk to Dad more often, sometimes more than once a day. I don't think they have much trust in Mom. The real estate agent has also brought a few prospective buyers through the house. It's no surprise to me that she hasn't received any offers. For one thing, the damage Chase caused during his break-in is still not repaired. But more importantly, to an outsider, the atmosphere in the house must feel as cold and indifferent as a chain-link fence.

Every day I take the bus to the secondhand shop to visit my guitar. On my third visit it's no longer in the window. My heart misses a couple of beats. But once I am inside and find it hanging with others along the wall, I breathe a sigh of relief.

The clerk looks up from his crossword puzzle. "Are you ready to buy?"

"Not unless the price has come way down."

"A couple of hundred perhaps. Say, twelve hundred."

I shake my head. "I can't do it." I am about to leave, but I have a thought. "I'm just curious, how much did you give my brother for it?"

He eyes me suspiciously. "Your brother didn't sell it to me."

"Maybe you just don't remember." I speak as calmly as my emotions will allow. "You must make a lot of deals in a day. He's skinny, his hair is brown, and he has sores all over his face. He looks pretty much like every other drug addict. He stole it. He punched a hole in my closet where I kept it locked up."

The clerk silently considers his puzzle. He then repeats what he'd told me the first time I came in. "I told you, I bought it from a woman."

But he hasn't said it fast enough or in a way that is at all convincing. I know now, for certain, that he bought it from Chase.

"Okay, how much was it worth to her?"

"She got a fair price." He slides the pencil behind an ear. "What makes you so sure it's yours, anyway?"

"I bought it. I played it for six months. I recognize my own guitar." I leave the store.

The following day the price drops another hundred dollars. And the day after that, the last day of school, one hundred more. It has also been moved to the back of the store where it looks like old stock.

Jack, Steve and Bobby are keen on practicing more now that school is out. At least for them it's out. I start summer school on Monday. It runs every morning until the end of July, which at least allows me to work in the afternoons and save some money. The battle of the bands is the first weekend in August.

The three of them have played a few times since Chase took off with my guitar. They've been using an electronic keyboard to replace me, hoping a miracle will happen before August and I'll find a new bass. Jack complains after every practice.

"It sucks," he tells me. "We'd have a dirtier sound if we brought my little sister in to replace you."

I try to brace myself for the announcement that they have found a new bass player and I'm out of The Pogos. It has to come; they won't qualify to play in the battle of the bands without live musicians.

Saturday morning, Jack asks me to come over and listen to what they've been working on. When I arrive, Steve and Bobby are already there, playing pool in the basement. Their equipment fills the adjoining space. Steve takes a last shot while Jack tells me he's worked out most of the riffs to the Foo Fighters tune we'd been learning to play.

"We want you to listen. But first we want to show you something." He sets down his guitar. He's acting a little strange, goofy somehow.

"All right, what?"

Jack pulls a guitar case out from under the old plaid couch. He lays it on top of the cushions, which are tattered from his cats sharpening their claws.

The case has also seen better days. It's beat-up and one latch is broken.

"What's this?"

"Open it." Steve and Bobby have racked their pool cues and are standing next to us, waiting.

I open it. Inside is a bottom line, Indonesian-made bass. It's sure nothing compared to my P-bass but it's in decent condition. I lift it from the case.

"Okay, we know it's sort of a piece of crap. But it's what we could afford when we threw our money together. It'll do for a while, at least to practice."

Jack doesn't need to apologize. Instead of getting someone to replace me, they'd gone and done this. I can't believe it. I play a few notes. "It's great. With a new set of strings it will be even better. I don't know what else to say but thanks."

We have a fantastic practice, driving through one song after another and not breaking until one in the morning. It's like when we'd first started to play as a band and actually made it through a whole song. We choose the three songs we will play in the first round of the battle of the bands.

Walking home, carrying my new beat-up case, it feels good to be a Pogo again.

In the awful days following Chase's escape, Dad sleep-walks through life. He gets up in the morning and goes to work. He spends the evenings in his study, marking papers or, more often than not, just staring at the wall. He says little to me, but I've noticed that I do seem to be his little bridge to sanity, even though I hardly feel all that sane myself. I say this because if he sees me pass down the hallway, he'll sit up at his desk like he's just woken up. "How are our groceries?" he'll ask, or, "Did the paper come today?"

I know he really doesn't care if the paper has come or not. He hasn't looked at it in weeks. No, I think he asks about these ordinary things just to assure himself that the normal world is still turning outside our closed and chaotic one. Or it could be that his thoughts while pondering the wall have spun wildly out of control and he needs something to grab on to, to steady himself.

As for me, I try to spend as little time as I can at home. I have thought a lot about what Detective Keppler told me about not letting Chase suck me in too. If I have to be a jerk and ignore what's going on around me, I've decided that's what I'm going to do. On the other hand, it's fairly easy, because nothing's happened. Chase has gone underground.

It takes a good deal of pressure off Dad just having Aunt Gail around. Mom still cries most of the time. The rest of her time is absorbed in trying to come up with a plan to help Chase. Although her ideas are more like ridiculous schemes than rational plans. For example, she figures if she could only find Chase, she could get him into a clinic in some other country. Aunt Gail listens, then tries to reason with her—something Dad and I gave up on some time ago.

With summer school every day I don't see much of Jade outside of work. Her mother is in a special clinic for a couple of weeks. She's being assessed for some kind of new treatment, so Jade is spending a lot of time with Holly. It's good for her and she seems more relaxed without the strain of caring for her mom. Still, she is looking forward to her mother coming home, because her aunt, who lives in Seattle, has arranged a sitter for Holly and homecare for her mom. Jade and her friend, Laura, can then visit Seattle for a week. I sure am going to miss her, but for her sake, I know a change of scenery will be good.

Sitting in summer school class with Jason Dodds and Brian Zimmerman feels like I'm part of some moronic reality show. I do my best to ignore them. I keep my head down and my mouth shut. I've also got into the routine of doing my homework in the library before I go to work. If I stick to this system, I should be able to make it through July.

I'm not so sure that Mr. Saik will make it, though. In the first few days, I see him quietly count to ten every time Dodds shouts out some idiotic remark. But it's hot, the sound of little kids playing in the wading pool in the park next to the school grounds drifts through the open window, and every day at 10:00 o'clock he has to compete with the ice-cream truck blaring some jolly tune. Even he gazes outside now and again, no doubt wishing he were somewhere else. After a few days, he loses patience with Dodds and begins barking back at him the instant he opens his mouth.

Thursday evening I get my paycheck. Six more weeks and I can afford to buy back my guitar. On Friday I have no homework after school and enough time before work to make my daily trek to the pawn-shop. My guitar has been moved again. Not only that, it's plugged into an amplifier. I lift it from the guitar stand.

"Someone was playing it," I comment out loud.

The clerk is sorting through a pile of old coins. "Yup, I got an offer."

My stomach drops.

"Don't worry. As you can see, it's still here. I told him I'd think about it."

There is still hope, but I doubt there is very much. "What was the offer?"

The clerk wipes his hands on a dirty rag. "I'm not sure how that's your business. But I'll tell you anyway. He offered me one grand."

"But that's what you said you're asking the last time I was in."

"That's what I told you I wanted. I told him my original price, fifteen hundred."

For whatever reason I seem to be getting special consideration. Maybe the guy is more human than his business makes him seem. "I got paid today. It's still going to be a few weeks, but I'm saving everything. Will you hang on to it for me, even if he comes back at that price?"

"Like I told you before, I'm a business, not a charity. I'll decide when and if he comes back."

He swipes the separated piles of coins from the counter into boxes while I play one of the songs we've been rehearsing on my bass. I'm about to set it down when the door opens and a guy, probably in his mid-twenties, enters the store. He carries a stereo amplifier. The cords drag behind him and the plug bounces across the floor as he crosses the room. After setting the amplifier on the counter next to the clerk's boxes he mutters, "How much?" His hair is long but thin with a yellow waxy patch of skin showing through the top.

The clerk makes a point of moving the coins out of his reach. As he does, his customer glances behind and around him. There is no mistaking the paranoid darting eyes of an addict.

"Where did you get it?"

The addict shrugs as he runs a hand beneath his nose. He has trouble coming up with an immediate answer. Finally he says, "I got all the equipment I need. I got a new one. I don't need this one anymore."

It's a decent amplifier, not a piece of junk, probably around five hundred dollars new.

"Does it work?" The clerk wiggles the cords, testing for obvious loose connections.

"Like a charm. It's brand new. Worth at least three hundred."

The clerk glances quickly at him when he quotes the price but says nothing as he turns it over. He's studying the small silver plate stamped with a serial number. Something else catches his eye. He flips the piece of equipment upright again. "Sorry, I can't take it."

"Okay, one hundred. But you know it's worth more than that."

"Look, buddy, it's not worth anything to me. It's engraved with the name of a school. It's stolen property, and I'm not buying it."

Stuffing his hands in his pockets, the thin man doesn't reply right away but paces before the counter. He's clearly agitated. I doubt it's at the prospect of dropping the price further, but more likely because he might not be shooting up within the next fifteen minutes like he'd anticipated when he'd walked through the door.

His pace quickens. My skin jumps when he turns suddenly and slams his fist on the counter. "Are you calling me a thief?"

Appearing unperturbed, the clerk leans forward. "I'm not calling you anything—yet. I said this piece of equipment belongs to the school engraved on the back. See this: WSS Music Department. I don't know how you got it, and I frankly don't care. But I'm not giving you money unless you can produce a document with that same name on it. Now get out of here."

The man lifts his palms in the air in a gesture of submission. "All right, all right. You win. I'll take fifty, no less." It's an effort for him to slow down and try to sound reasonable. Beads of sweat appear on his forehead.

"You'll take nothing, like I said. Now get out of here." The clerk begins moving the coin boxes to shelves, indicating the conversation is over.

The addict remains planted where he is, unsure of what to do, wanting that fix. He walks to the door without the amplifier, then back to the counter again. "Okay, yeah, I got it from the Dumpster behind the school. I don't know why they'd throw out a perfectly good amp, but they did. Twenty bucks and it's yours. Come on, twenty bucks, that's nothing to you. I need it for my mother. She's sick. She can't stop coughing. She's on welfare because of a bad hip that won't let her work."

"Get going, buddy—now—or I'll have to have you removed." The clerk picks up the phone in a threat to call the police.

I don't move. I'm not sure how I can help or why I should care—but it doesn't seem right to walk off and leave anyone alone with a nutjob like that. I flick the switch on the amplifier off; the sound cracks in the air.

The addict turns. For the first time, his eyes fall on me.

"Take it," the clerk orders, pushing the amplifier toward him. "Try the flea market."

The addict looks me over. He then turns back to the counter, picks up the amplifier and leaves. Once the door has closed behind him I move to set my bass back on the guitar stand where I'd found it. It dawns on me that I'm holding it like a weapon. When had I raised it, ready to swing if he'd become violent? I place it on the stand and turn to leave.

"Where do you work?" The clerk sets the last box of coins on the shelf behind him.

"Barnes Hardware."

"Huh, you're in retail too. Ever run into customers like that?"

I shrug. "There's the odd difficult one, yeah. But we don't see any like that."

After opening a drawer beneath the shelf, he pulls out a stack of tickets, shuffles through them and removes one. "You said you got paid today. How much was your paycheck?"

"Two hundred and fifty dollars. Like I told you, I'll have the money in six more weeks."

He leans forward, propping his elbows on the counter, still holding the ticket. "Is the money from your paycheck in the bank?"

"Yeah," I say. "Why?"

"I'll take two hundred dollars for that guitar. If you pay me now, you can take it with you."

I don't know what to say.

"Well, take it or leave it. I'm not going to give you a better price. That's what I gave your brother."

"You paid my brother two hundred—for my P-bass?"

"What was I supposed to do? He took my first offer. He grabbed the cash and didn't even wait for the ticket. Should I have said 'Hang on, I'd like to give you more'?"

"Of course not." I dig my bank card from out of my pocket.

Once he has put my card through and debited my account, he hands it back to me. "Good, there you go, it's all yours. Thanks for your business. Now, take your guitar and keep it in a safe place."

THIRTEEN

The next week passes quickly. I am rarely home during the day. I'm either at school or work, and since I got my P-bass back, The Pogos practice every night. Most nights I don't get home until one or two o'clock in the morning. I often find Dad asleep in the chair in front of the TV. Even in sleep, his face doesn't relax. Chase never leaves his mind. He may show up in his dreams as some strange creature he can't get away from or maybe some weird situation he's stuck in, but it will still be Chase. Rather than wake him up, I throw a blanket over him, turn off the TV and switch off the lights.

On a Saturday morning in mid-July, Detective Keppler sits at our kitchen table and tells Dad that he's frustrated. Mom is not around. Aunt Gail has insisted on taking her to have her hair done. She told Mom that even if she didn't care what she looked like, we do. When that didn't convince her, she told her she was taking her anyhow.

Detective Keppler is confident that they'll get Chase eventually. He's just frustrated that it's taking so long. In the meantime, he's been taking some heat from Richard Cross's family, who don't understand how it can be so difficult to bring in a drug addict. How could an entire police force be given the slip by a high school dropout with scrambled brains? He doesn't actually say this. He's much kinder, but in fact I know that's what Richard Cross's family means.

"They don't understand how these guys work. Chase has probably been in one place since he ran. I doubt that he's moved very much. We've been out day and night asking questions, but none of the regulars on the streets have seen him, and he hasn't used any of the shelters or accessed community services. So far, he's left nothing for us to trace."

All I know is that I wouldn't want to be in the detective's position, going back and forth between two families, one dealing with a murder in the family, the other dying a slow death.

He is certain that Chase will surface when he gets desperate enough, like when he began calling Mom from the drug store. It's just a matter of when that will be.

It turns out to be the following day. It's a Sunday, and I am working alone at the hardware store. Ralph has taken the entire day off, leaving me in charge like he's been training me to do, and Jade is visiting her aunt in Seattle for a few days. It's a warm sunny day and business has been slow since I opened at noon. People would rather be out in the sun than inside, unclogging their drains.

It's around three o'clock when I hear the jingle of the bell attached to the door. I am moving boxes in the storeroom. Wiping my hands on my jeans, I walk through the doorway to the front of the store. At first I think I am seeing things. A ghost is coming toward the counter. It's running toward me: a skeleton covered in jaundiced skin. Quick and spastic, it has started talking before I realize it's my brother. Still, I can't stop staring at this weird and jerky marionette. There are deep hollows where his cheeks used to be and his arms—dangling from the sleeves of his T-shirt—are freakishly thin. A ripe odor makes me take a step back when he comes up close.

"Gordie, I need money. Five hundred." As he speaks, his eyes sweep the store in a paranoid way.

"Chase?" I recognize him, yet I can't take my eyes from him. He is missing more teeth, and the sores on his face are infected. So are the tracks on his arms. I don't respond to what he says immediately, because I am trying to comprehend how it can be that this—this withered human standing before me—is why my mother is ready for a mental hospital. He is the reason my father is selling the house. He is the cause of all the arguing and cruel words that have passed between us. Everything my parents owned, everything I had saved for, everything we had been, has been sucked into the wasted vortex that is Chase.

"They're going to kill me if I don't get it."

"Who's going to kill you?"

"Ratchet and DC." Chase turns and glances over his shoulder toward the street.

I follow his gaze. Through the window I spot the black Passat parked next to the curb, right in front of the store. Ratchet leans lazily against the car, waiting.

As soon as I see the car, the strange feeling that his appearance is a nightmare lifts and my adrenaline kicks in. "You idiot!" I reach over and grab the neck of his filthy T-shirt. "What did you bring them here for?" I barely touch him, but he loses his balance and falls back into a shelf of belt sanders.

"I didn't. They drove me here. They said they knew where I could get the money."

I gape at Chase and his hollow stare. Acid creeps up from my stomach, leaving a bitter taste in my mouth. I press the palms of my hands hard against the counter. "I already gave you all my money, you freak. Or have you smoked that memory away with everything else?"

Chase starts toward the cash register. "Come on, there's got to be a lot of cash in here. Open it. You must have at least five hundred. I'll pay you back."

"You'll pay me back? Get away from there. That's not my money."

It all happens so fast that I have to think quickly. It crosses my mind that I could give him the money and then call Detective Keppler, but I've already played that part and it was a total bust. He can't be trusted even for a matter of seconds, and what if he does take off and the cops lose the Passat when they take after them? It's bad enough to lose my own money. I can't risk Ralph's, not to mention my job and everything that goes along with it.

I also consider tackling him and pinning him down while I call the police. But Ratchet and DC are watching. If they see me make a move toward Chase or the phone, they'll come busting in.

I can come up with only one solution. I walk toward the front door at my regular pace so as not to alarm Ratchet. I turn the dead bolt. Ratchet looks up.

"What are you doing?" Chase's eyes skitter between me and the door.

"I'm giving you a choice. They won't kill you if they can't get their hands on you."

"Is there another way out?" He looks in the direction of the doorway to the storeroom, the one I had come through.

I close that door and lock it with my key. "Yeah, but it's not through here. Listen to me. This is what I'm going to do. Ratchet and DC can't get in. I'm going to call the police, and I'm going to keep the front door locked until they get here. You sit down and just wait. It's the only way. They're going to get you sooner or later. You'll have to go to jail, but if you go back out on the street—if you go out to Ratchet without the money now—you said yourself that you're as good as dead."

As I speak, Chase's eyes grow wide. I should have known that he was tweaking. Every muscle twitches and his eyes quiver as he tries to process what I have said. I don't know what he hears, but I immediately realize that I shouldn't have told him my plan. I already know well enough there is no reasoning with a drug addict, especially one that's been pumped for four or five days and now wants nothing more in the world than that next hit. Trapped and knowing it, he reacts with the same animal instincts he's been running on since he'd first taken off.

He lunges toward the cash register. I watch him struggle with it before drawing the key from the pocket of my jeans. "That's locked too. Do what I say. You've really got no choice." I try to be slow and casual when I pick up the phone. "I'm going to call Detective Keppler. He's an okay guy. He's the one that's been following you."

At the same time as I pick up the phone, I scan the shelves close to me. I spot a rubber mallet within my reach. I don't know just how buzzed he is, but I know he'll do pretty much anything to get away, including attack me. I punch in the detective's cell number. Eating alone in the kitchen over the last few weeks, staring at his card on the fridge every night, it's now burned into my brain.

It's while I'm dialing that Chase does the one thing I never expected he would do. He bolts to the front of the store where he turns the dead bolt. He tears out onto the street. He tries to get by Ratchet, who sticks his foot in Chase's path and trips him. Ratchet grips him by the arm.

The detective answers just before I drop the phone and take off after Chase. Through the window I can see Ratchet speaking to Chase as I head for the door—I guess he is asking if he has the money. He then begins pummeling Chase on the side of his head and drags him across the sidewalk. I can hear the solid, unrestrained blows through the closed door. As I open it, Ratchet shoves Chase into the backseat. He jumps in next to him, and the car roars off.

I stand on the sidewalk, looking after them. I want to scream. I have no way to go after them. I should have punched Chase out myself when I had him standing in front of me. Just to keep him from running. Just to keep him from getting killed.

I return to the store where I can't even think of
work. I pace the floor, trying to think of what to do next.
I hate him. He's ruined my life, and he's ruined Mom
and Dad's. But the sound of Ratchet's fist whacking his
head will not leave my brain. I hate him for everything
he's done, but still, I don't want him to be dead. I just
want it all to end. I kick the counter. What had I been
thinking? Of course, Chase would risk taking off with
Ratchet. They might pound him into unconsciousness,
but at least there was the chance for another hit. If he
went to jail there would be absolutely none at all.

I am suddenly aware of the drone of the telephone,
telling me it is disconnected. I pick it up and dial
Detective Keppler's number again. He answers right
away. I try to explain what has happened. "I couldn't
stop him," I finish. "I was calling you, and he just ran."

"Okay," he says, "I'll be right there."

Within minutes I hear sirens nearing Barnes
Hardware store. I wish they blended in with all the
other sounds of the street like they always have, but
because I know why they are coming, they roar inside
my head. There are soon three or four cars wailing.

A police cruiser pulls up in front of the building
and two cops jump out. I meet them at the front door.
I confirm the direction the Passat had been going
when they ask. They walk through every aisle of the
store before checking the storeroom. Did they think I

was lying, that I was actually hiding Chase? They are headed back to their car when another cruiser pulls up behind them. Detective Keppler steps out of the front passenger seat.

"Did you check inside the store?"

One of the cops nods. "Nothing."

The detective spots me. "Gordie, did you see the car actually drive off with Chase?"

"Yes," I say. "They pushed him into the backseat. They beat him up pretty good first."

"Okay, I've sent out cars to try and head them off. I'll let you know as soon as we know anything ourselves. You guys stay here in case they come back."

The two police officers that had showed up first return to their cruiser, where they sit and survey the street. I return to the empty store. A single customer comes in five minutes later. I am so distracted when he asks if we have any rubber gaskets that I tell him I think so, but I can't remember where, and he leaves.

Fifteen minutes pass, and I wonder if Chase is already dead. I do know that if Ratchet had continued pounding on him, it wouldn't take much. I debate calling Dad and letting him know what is going on, but I don't know how to tell him. I really can't face Mom. I've blown it so badly, I can hardly face myself.

I would lock up and go home—I'm sure if Ralph Barnes knew the circumstances he wouldn't blame me—but I have never told him anything about Chase. And anyway, for now, I'm safe. I don't have to hear about what I should have done and what was I thinking, and that it's my fault again that Chase might be dead.

Half an hour later, the police cruiser parked in front of the store drives off. And fifteen minutes after that, Detective Keppler pulls up.

He smiles a little as he saunters up the aisle to the front counter where I sit. I think it's meant to be encouraging, but it's too sad and it doesn't work. "How are you doing, Gordie?"

"Terrible. Did you find them?"

"Those two creeps got away from us in the car, but we tracked them down at a house in Burnaby." Flipping open a lawn chair, he sits across from me.

"And Chase?"

The detective shakes his head. "He wasn't with them. At first they denied everything you said. They said they hadn't been anywhere near the store this afternoon and they didn't know what we were talking about."

Anger burns in my chest. "They're lying."

"Yes, I know. When we told them that we had witnesses who saw them drag Chase into the car, they eventually agreed that they had been here. They remembered even more when we told them that because Chase was wanted for murder, they'd be implicated in that too if they didn't spit up. They said that yes,

Chase had been with them, that they had stopped at the store, but that he'd run out on them at an intersection two blocks after they'd left."

I recalled the image of Chase being punched and dragged into the car by Ratchet. He'd been in the backseat with him when they drove off.

"I don't believe that. Chase was out of it. Yeah, he was strung out, but after a few belts to the head he wouldn't have had the strength to fight back. He wouldn't have been able to run even if they'd opened the door and shoved him out."

Detective Keppler nods. "I'm not so sure I believe them either. But I've seen these guys when they're jacked up, and they can do things you wouldn't believe. Anyway, at this point, that's what we know."

"Are you going to keep looking?"

"We've never stopped." He smiles a little again as he stands up. "Now, why don't you close this place up and go home."

I shake my head. "I can't."

"Of course you can. The boss isn't in, how's he going to know?"

I find myself smiling too, but it fades quickly. "I can't go home because I don't know what I'm going to tell Mom and Dad. I had Chase here, and I let him get away. They'll be furious, and if he's dead, they'll say I drove him to it. He ran out the door because of what I did."

"Hey now, Gordie, you can't think like that." The detective sits down again. "If that's how Chase ends up—and we still don't know how it's all going to end—it's because of everything he did. Not you. Not your Mom or Dad. Your Mom and Dad are good people. They had you, didn't they?"

"Big deal."

"It is a big deal. It's a very big deal to them. But I'll tell you what, if it makes you feel better for now, I won't say anything for a few days. I have a strong hunch we'll have Chase soon. He made a very big mistake today. He's burned his bridges with his regular dealers and he's about as desperate as he can get."

"If he's still alive."

Detective Keppler ignores my comment. "The last time we talked, after Chase ran from the shopping center, what did I tell you then?"

I shrug. "Go to school. Do stuff with my friends."

"And, are you doing those things?"

"I'm trying."

"What about the girlfriend part? Do you have one?"

I wonder if he sees me blush. "I have a close friend that's a girl."

"What's she like?"

I think about how to describe Jade. There are so many great things about her, that it's tough to pick just one or two. "She's smart. She's kind. And she makes me laugh.

I can't really figure out why she likes me, though."

Detective Keppler laughs. "Well, I can. And if she makes you laugh, hang on to her." He stands up to leave again, folds the chair and puts it back on the stack. "Go home and call her, Gordie. Try to forget about what happened today. Perhaps tomorrow we'll have Chase and we can all move on from there."

Once he's gone, I turn out the lights and lock the store. Sitting on the bus on the way home I scan the streets for Chase. I feel exhausted and I have a headache, like I've been used as a punching bag. I wonder again if Chase is lying somewhere, dead. If he is, how long will it take before we know about it? Maybe his body will wash up on the shores of the Fraser River in a week, smashed from crashing up against the rocks so that nobody can tell how he really died. Or maybe he'll be one of those decomposed bodies stumbled on by a jogger in Stanley Park years from now.

Like Detective Keppler said, I have to stop thinking like that. For the remainder of the bus ride, I force myself to practice a Nickleback tune over and over again in my head. When I get home, I head straight to my room. I flip open my cell and dial Jade's number.

"Hey," I say when she answers. "When did you get back from Seattle?"

"Hey, Gordie, what's up? We got in about an hour ago. How was your weekend?"

"Never mind about mine, how was yours?"

"It was good. My aunt lives in an old house near the university. We spent yesterday at the market."

I'm not sure if she's finished, but I can't wait any longer. I have to say what I have called to say. "Listen, Jade, I want to ask you something. On Friday night, I was wondering if you'd like to do something with me? I was thinking we could go out for dinner to a nice place, and then after that, a movie or something. We both have it off work."

When Jade doesn't answer right away I get a little nervous. But then she says, "I'd love to, Gordie. I'd love to go out, just you and me."

FOURTEEN

Ryan is out of rehab. Jack tells me his parents are keeping a pretty tight rein on him since he got out, and he has strict orders not to socialize with any of his old friends. Because his mother knows the manager of the local grocery store well, she was able to get him a job bagging groceries for the summer. Her plan is that he will return to school in the fall and take extra classes at night school to get caught up on what he'd missed during the time that he'd been strung out.

I am happy for Ryan, but I have to admit that deep down, I do wish it were Chase. Instead, I'm searching the newspaper every day for some kind of clue as to where he is: an unidentified body turned up somewhere or a violent accident where the victim isn't named. I sometimes wonder how many other people are doing the same thing. I also wonder how many actually go down to the morgue to view the unidentified bodies on the chance that they could end the agony of not knowing.

If Chase isn't dead, I can only imagine how he's managing to survive. He would have been cut off by Ratchet and DC, there is no question about that. He would have had to find a new dealer, although I doubt he would have had to look too far. I keep thinking of the junkie that I'd passed when I was searching for my bass. The one who was peddling sex for a fix. If he is still alive, Chase is that low too; he is one of those guys.

I hadn't told anyone but Jade that he had come into the store. She'd tried to convince me that I'd handled it the right way.

"Think of the alternatives," she'd said. "If you'd given him the money, Ralph would have been out five hundred dollars, and you would have been fired. If you'd simply refused and started an argument with him, told him to get out, he might have become violent, and who knows how that might have ended up."

I do sometimes wonder why he never made a move to knock me out with something and grab the key to the cash register. It wasn't beyond what he would do; history has proven that. Maybe somewhere in the tangled neurons of his pitted brain he'd known it was me. Maybe something told him I wasn't to be harmed because at one time I'd meant something to him. It would be nice to believe that.

Mom and Dad hardly talk to me anymore, let alone to each other. They are like ghosts sliding around, in and out of the house. Aunt Gail had insisted on taking Mom to the doctor to get something to cope with the stress. Rather than helping her to relax, whatever the doctor gave her has turned her cold and numb. I have also discovered that Dad has taken to knocking back a few drinks every night. I wasn't aware of it at first. But now I notice his eyes become glassy earlier and earlier in the evening as he sits at his desk in the den. Chase has managed to get both of them hooked.

The only time the whole mess doesn't eat away at my gut is when I am practicing with the band. With my friends around and my P-bass back, I can stay focused. For the rest of July, I practically live at Jack's while we practice like crazy for the battle of the bands. After a month of nightly practices we are pretty tight, and we have developed a real gritty sound.

I make it through summer school. It's a relief to pass, but it's more of a relief to know I won't have to spend any time within the same two hundred square feet as Dodds and Zimmerman for at least another month.

Finally, over the first weekend of August we compete with other bands from the North Shore. It's the coolest thing I've ever done. The auditorium is packed with kids from high schools all over Vancouver. At the end of the afternoon they vote, and we can't believe it when we make second place. We didn't think we'd place at

all after hearing some of the other bands play. Steve and
Bobby say it was because I kept them solid, but I think
we sold them on our second song when Jack did this
John Frusciante-thing with his guitar. The crowd really
went nuts for the wild clunky sound. After it is over, bass
players come up to me and ask me about specific riffs
and how I'd come up with the sound. I really don't know
what to say, other than to show them. I tell them it was
just a matter of figuring it out and then playing it over
and over until it came out the way it did. And, while I
was playing it, not thinking of anything else. At the end
of the day we have two invitations to play at schools in
September. It's one of the sweetest days of my life.

Two days later, I buy a sub sandwich after getting
off the bus at the mall. I walk home and sit down in
front of the TV to eat it. The news is on and there is a
story of some guy who had stolen a car at the Capilano
Shopping Center and led the police on a high-speed
chase earlier in the day. The car was a red Honda Civic,
and it belonged to a woman with two little kids. She'd
stopped for five minutes, she said, to run into the drug
store to pick up some cough medicine for one of her
kids. There is a video clip of her standing in the rain in
the parking lot. She has a baby in her arms, and a kid
with a runny nose is clinging to her jeans.

An hour after the woman reported her car missing,
the cops spotted it heading east along the Upper Levels

Highway toward the Second Narrows Bridge. When they turned on the siren, the driver picked up speed. He led them across the bridge, at 150 kilometers an hour, and along the freeway. More police cars and a police helicopter joined the chase. The guy was nearing the west end of the Port Mann Bridge when the cops blew his tires and blocked him in. Surrounded by five police cruisers and with six guns pointed at his head, he was ordered out of the car. Despite the order, his head fell forward against the steering wheel, and he didn't open the door.

The reporter explains that the reason for this was because in the seconds before the police got out of their cars, he swallowed something which was later identified as a large amount of drugs. Why he did it was a mystery. It didn't make sense that he would try to hide the fact that he was carrying drugs, considering the trouble he was already in. One officer guessed that he wanted a last hit before he was arrested. He'd seen it before.

When he didn't move, the cops opened the door and pulled him out of the car. He was still conscious. They slammed him to the ground. The footage they show on TV is of the guy lying on his stomach on the shoulder of the highway, surrounded by police officers, one of them cinching handcuffs on his wrists, which are clasped behind his back. The guy's face is not visible in the shot. His takedown looked pretty violent, but adrenaline was running high and all the police knew was that he'd stolen a car and was running from them. They had no idea who he was, what he'd done, or if he was carrying a weapon.

The film clip ends and the reporter goes on to say that minutes after he was apprehended the thief went into cardiac arrest. His eyes rolled back in his head and he stopped breathing. The same cops that had cuffed him so tightly, pumped hard on his chest in an effort to keep him alive. An ambulance was called, and he was rushed to the hospital. They tried to get his heart beating regularly again, but it took some time. He was now in critical condition in intensive care. His name cannot be released until the family has been notified, and then an investigation will be completed. The reporter moves on to the next story. I turn off the TV and finish my sandwich.

I hadn't seen his face. I had only seen his body lying in the gravel on the shoulder of the highway through the legs of a dozen cops, but I knew it was Chase.

Three hours later, Detective Keppler knocks on our front door. He takes Mom and Dad to the hospital. The doctors tell them that the lack of oxygen when Chase went into cardiac arrest has caused irreversible damage to his already severely drug-damaged organs. Only time will tell how much.

When I ask Dad if Chase is going to live, he says, "We won't know anything for sure, not for a few days."

My parents spend every hour of the next two days at the hospital. I don't want to see Chase. I can't explain why. When they do come home, Dad is in a fog, although somehow calmer than I have seen him in a long time, maybe because he knows where Chase is. Mom is a total wreck. She is furious with the police for being so rough. Despite the doctors telling her that the bruises on his head are old bruises, that they were not the result of his arrest, she blames the police for the way he looks.

My mother's parents fly in from Ontario. They didn't know Chase had taken off or that Richard Cross had died. They didn't know the house was up for sale or that Mom and Dad had all but split up. Everything about the way we have been living is news to them, and they are appalled. I really don't need their constant moans of disbelief as they discover some new aspect of our dysfunctional lives. I am already quite aware of how abnormal we have become.

When I do visit Chase, it's on the morning of the third day that he's in the hospital. It's before anyone else has arrived. Dad knows I'm going. He has told me I should go soon because things are not looking good. I guess I've been putting it off because I still feel so angry at him. I resent him for everything he's done and has put us through. I wanted to get over that a bit first, so if he does happen to regain consciousness when I'm in the room, the first thing I do won't be to punch him out. But I am scared I won't be able to stop myself.

Dad stops me before I leave the house. "I want to warn you, Gordie. He doesn't look anything like he used to. He's very thin. The drugs and his life on the street have been hard on him. I'm telling you just in case you expect him to look like your brother used to. I don't want you to be too shocked."

Chase looks exactly like he did when he'd come into the hardware store except for the yellow-green bruises on his temple, the marks on his wrists left by the hand-cuffs and the road burn on his face. He is, in fact, a wasted and battered shell of something that was once human. I expect to feel a lot more than I do when I lay eyes on him, but I don't feel much of anything at all.

Mostly I am overwhelmed with sadness and anger. It's all just such a waste. Everything and everyone connected to Chase is broken. And I wonder, why did he have to go running out of the store when I was trying to help him? Why did he choose those two scumbags over me?

Two days later, the doctors tell my parents that Chase is brain dead. There is no electrical activity in his brain and there never will be again. They suggest that my parents should consider disconnecting Chase from the life support system.

I don't go to the hospital on the day it is disconnected. Instead I wander aimlessly around the house,
walking from one room to the next, wondering if I'll
feel anything the moment he dies. Later, when Dad tells
me the approximate time, I realize that I hadn't. I then
go into my room, and for the first time since he'd been
in the hospital, I sit down on my bed and bawl.

It is now the middle of October. Our house sold at the
end of August. It was bought by a young family with
two little girls. The deal was that the buyers would meet
the full asking price if we could be out by October first.
The real estate agent was excited to have made the sale.
She told Dad one of the first things the new family was
going to do was change the color of the bedrooms in
the basement. The ones, she'd said, that you'd painted
for your boys.

Dad and I are now living in a two-bedroom walk-up
apartment behind the local mall. He didn't want to move
too far away from where I'd grown up, for my sake.
He didn't want to make too many changes too quickly,
particularly in my last year of high school. With everything else that has happened, he didn't want me to get
stressed-out. In the end, he could have hung on to the
house, since there would be no large fees owing to lawyers,
but he thought it best that we try for a fresh start.

Dad has about one good day out of seven. Well, even that one is not really all that good, it's just not as bad as all the rest. He cries a lot. But he's doing better than during the first month after Chase died, when he didn't have any good days at all. Grandma and Aunt Gail have us over for supper a couple of times a week, so at least he's eating.

I'm not really sure how Mom is coping. My grandparents took her back to Ontario, where they are trying to help her out. She phoned twice this week, which I see as a good sign. The second time, after she'd finished speaking with Dad, she asked him to put me on the line. She wanted to know how our gig in Deep Cove went. I was impressed that she had even remembered that I'd told her we had a gig, which could mean she's starting to think of things other than what has happened over the last two years.

I try hard to stay positive and focus on my own life, like Detective Keppler told me to do, but it's not always easy. At the weirdest times I get flashes of things that happened in the past two years. Like yesterday when I was doing my homework and an image of Richard Cross's little girl came into my head. I saw her being pulled across the lobby of the hospital and the unicorn flying out of her hand. I saw her mother walking with determination.

But the flashback I get most often is about the day Chase came into the store. If he'd only stayed with me, things could have turned out so differently. I've followed that image through and played it out differently. I've imagined that he does stay with me and waits for the cops to arrive. He still goes to jail in my vision, but he's also still alive. But that didn't happen, and I can't change it. I gave him a choice, and he took the one I never thought he would.

Once in a while, I drop in to Ms. Larson's office. She asked me if I would, so she could help make sure I don't lose focus at school. When I told her about what happened in the hardware store that day she said, "Just think about that for a minute. Yes, you gave him a choice. But who made the choices that put Chase at the hardware store?"

"I guess Chase did."

"Yes, and when you look back at everything that's happened, who was making the choices all along?"

I got the point.

"Gordie, everyone did what they could to get him on the right track. But when it comes right down to it, we are the navigators of our own lives."

I am reminded of what she said when I bump into Ryan Linscott at the shopping mall. His mother had so many plans for him. Ryan is standing outside the drug store, waiting for someone while I am headed into the store to pick up a couple of things for Dad. He doesn't strike me as looking all that good, but I figure it will take some time to put the weight back on and maybe even longer to bring some life back into his vacant eyes.

"Hey, Ryan," I say. "Good to see you."

He turns. I don't think he recognizes me at first.

"Gord Jessup," I remind him.

"Oh, yeah, hey, Gordie." A look comes across his face like he's straining to remember something but he can't think of what it is.

"I hear you're working at the grocery store."

Ryan shakes his head. "Nah, not anymore. I gave that up. I'll get back to it, though. I've just got too many other things going on right now."

I nod. "How are you doing anyway?"

Ryan's eyes drift away from me. "Not bad. I'm doing okay." Suddenly remembering what he'd been straining for, he looks back to me. "Oh man, I was really sorry to hear about Chase. What a crappy way to end up."

"Yeah," I say. "Thanks. But you're doing good. I'm glad to hear it."

"Yeah," he says. And then in a familiar move, he rubs his nose with the back of his hand. "I'm doing all right."

I open the door to the drug store. I am about to go in when Ryan calls my name again.

"Gordie?"

I turn. "What's up?"

"Hey, I wouldn't normally ask, but I'm a little hard up right now. Could you loan me twenty bucks?"

KATHERINE HOLUBITSKY's first novel, *Alone at Ninety Foot* (Orca), won the CLA Book of the Year for Young Adults and the IODE Violet Downey Book Award. Since then, she has written *Last Summer in Agatha*, *The Hippie House*, *The Mountain that Walked* and *The Big Snapper*, all published by Orca. Katherine lives in Edmonton, Alberta, with her husband.